A Spy's Guide to Seduction

Books by Kate Moore

The Husband Hunter's Guide to London
A Lady's Guide to Passion and Property
A Spy's Guide to Seduction

A Spy's Guide to Seduction

Kate Moore

LYRICAL PRESS
Kensington Publishing Corp.
www.kensingtonbooks.com

LYRICAL PRESS BOOKS are published by

Kensington Publishing Corp.
119 West 40th Street
New York, NY 10018

All Kensington titles, imprints, and distributed lines are available at special quantity discounts for bulk purchases for sales promotion, premiums, fund-raising, educational, or institutional use.

Special book excerpts or customized printings can also be created to fit specific needs. For details, write or phone the office of the Kensington Sales Manager: Kensington Publishing Corp., 119 West 40th Street, New York, NY 10018. Attn. Sales Department. Phone: 1-800-221-2647.

Lyrical Press and Lyrical Press logo Reg. U.S. Pat. & TM Off.

First Electronic Edition: March 2019
ISBN-13: 978-1-5161-0178-8 (ebook)
ISBN-10: 1-5161-0178-2 (ebook)

First Print Edition: March 2019
ISBN-13: 978-1-5161-0179-5
ISBN-10: 1-5161-0179-0

Printed in the United States of America

To all the Violas and Rosalinds in their doublets and hose
who ever wanted to strap on a sword, take on the villain,
solve the mystery, and rescue the hero—
This one's for you.

Acknowledgments

I acknowledge my debt to Jane Austen without whom I would not have written any of the novels I have so far penned. It has been my aim from the beginning to hold myself to her high standards, though with zero claim to any of her genius. Among those standards was her ideal that her heroines should do only "the most natural, possible, everyday things" as they fall in love. They should call on their neighbors, dine with their families, and care for the people around them. They should be flawed and need to reflect in some mortification on their errors of judgment and resolve to do better. They should fall in love in the midst of imperfect families.

Nevertheless spies and villains will intrude in my stories in the wake of young men active in the world of the Napoleonic wars and their aftermath. So I hope that should I meet Ms. Austen at some gathering of writers in the hereafter, she will not entirely condemn my imperfect efforts but regard them as she did the work of her nieces Fanny and Anna.

I owe a further debt to writers like Amor Towles and Dickens, who insist that weather is always part of the story. For the weather in *A Spy's Guide to Seduction*, I used diaries and other accounts of actual English weather for the weeks in which the story occurs. By chance it turns out that as I was writing of thunder and lightning in 1826, London in 2018 experienced an extraordinary lightning storm.

Every detail of the story, including the missing papers, letters between the Persian ruler and his son, depends on research, and where research fails, I turned to friends like writer and horsewoman Laura Moore, and labor and delivery coach, doula Kara Humphreys, both of whom have saved me from error.

As always everything depends on my husband and children, my patient editor and savvy agent. Thanks to all.

Chapter One

Of all the gentlemen in London, the attractive rogue poses the greatest danger to the husband hunter's happiness.

—*The Husband Hunter's Guide to London*

Lady Emily Radstock accepted a greeting from her sister's butler, Gittings, and handed him her coat, gloves, and bonnet. She dispensed with Gittings's attempt to precede her up the stairs to the drawing room. He mumbled something as she bounded past him with her package under her arm. She assured him she did not need to be announced. Gittings was sixty if he was a day, and Emily was in a hurry.

As she threw open the drawing room door, her younger sister Rosalind, sitting at her needlework, her stocking feet on a blue velvet ottoman, looked up with a start.

"Where is she?" Emily demanded. The door closed behind her.

"Hello, Em. Where is who?" Rosalind held up a delicate white gown no bigger than a tea towel.

"Mother," said Emily. She strode across the room to stand before her sister, looking down. Rosalind, six years younger than Emily, and rosy and round with her first pregnancy, made a strikingly domestic appearance.

"Oh, Mother's gone to Grandmama's."

Emily sank onto the sofa opposite her sister. "Of all the cowardly dodges. She knows she's safe from me there."

"What's she done?" Rosalind asked, lowering the white garment to her lap.

"This!" said Emily, tossing the package she carried onto the small gateleg table next to Rosalind. The package made a satisfying slap against the polished wood.

Rosalind regarded it warily. "She's offended you with a brown paper package tied up in string."

"No. Yes. Come to think of it, I am offended by the brown paper and the string, her idea of being discreet before the servants."

"Em, you must enlighten me. I'm growing more confused by the minute."

"Sorry, Roz. Were you napping?" Emily realized that half the drapery over the tall windows had been drawn to shadow the far end of the room, where Rosalind had stationed the spectacular camel-backed sofa their mother had given her. Upholstered in a deep green and peony-patterned damask, the large sofa had been turned to face away from the delicate blues and golds of the room's main seating arrangement.

"No, I drew the drapery because—"

"How are you?" Emily leaned forward, looking closely at her sister.

"Quite well really. A great many of the discomforts have passed, and the terrible fatigue. That's why Mother thought she could go to Grandmama, who really does need her more than I do at the moment. And I have Philip," she said brightly.

"Is Phil much help?" Emily asked. "I didn't know husbands were."

"He is." Rosalind smiled in what Emily thought was a rather dreamy way for a married woman about to bear a child. "But you came to tell me what's upset you."

"Husbands. Or rather my lack of one and what mother chose to do about it. As if it were her problem. Open the package, Roz, you'll see."

"You know what's inside, Em?"

"I do. Open it."

Rosalind put aside her needlework and took up the little package, untying the string and pulling off the paper. She glanced at Emily and read the title on a small blue volume. "*The Husband Hunter's Guide to London?*"

"You see," said Emily, "wrapped up as if it were a gift and left for Alice to bring up with my chocolate this morning while Mama has gone off to avoid me."

"It's not a gift?" asked Rosalind, turning the pages of the little blue book, her gaze skimming over them.

"A gift?" Emily bounced a little on the sofa. "It's a notice to vacate. It's a shove out of the nest. It's a lit fuse on a bomb."

Rosalind looked up. "Surely, Mama means nothing of the kind."

"Doesn't she? It's my birthday in three weeks. I'll be twenty-nine. She considers me past hope, past praying for. Now she's given me a book for a schoolroom chit."

"Do you think so? You don't really want to continue at home, do you? You want an establishment of your own."

"Of course I do. But it won't be my establishment, will it? It will belong to some man, and it will be my job to run it for him."

Rosalind shook her head. "I don't think marriage...should be seen in exactly that light."

Emily stared at the rather magnificent painting of a chestnut stallion over the marble hearth. "You know, Roz, I should marry the first imbecile I meet, however brainless or idle he is."

"Darling, I don't think you should do anything so desperate."

The door to the sitting room opened, and a young man of fair, ruddy good looks, entered and stopped with a furrowed brow when he spotted Emily. "Hello, Em," he said. "I thought..." He looked around the room as if it were a puzzle to be solved.

"Phil, dear?" Rosalind gave him one of her dreamy smiles.

He crossed the room and gave his wife a quick kiss on the cheek. "Roz," he said, "I'm looking for Lynley. I thought Gittings said he showed him up to you, but now I find Em instead."

"Oh dear," said Roz. "I forgot all about Lynley."

"Where is he then?" Phil asked.

"Right here, old man." A deep voice came from the shadows, and a tall, dark-haired giant with a lean face, elegantly dressed limbs, and an indolent manner, unfolded himself from behind the camelback sofa. He fixed his gaze on Emily.

"You should have made yourself known, sir." Emily waited for her hair to catch on fire from the heat of the blush in her cheeks.

The giant moved her way with easy grace. "I think you've proposed to me," he said. "And I accept."

Emily had been trained all her life not to stare, but nothing could stop her from gaping up into the handsome, amused face staring down at her.

"Shall I put the announcement in the papers?" The giant took her hand in his large warm one, gave it a quick kiss, and turned to her brother-in-law. "At your service, Phil."

With a bow and a look of supreme satisfaction, he took his leave.

* * * *

Outside the townhouse on George Street, the two men headed south. It was a breezy, end-of-March day that required a man to fix his hat squarely on his head and lean into the wind. They had passed the blustery expanse of Grosvenor Square before Philip Villiers, Lord Woodford, spoke.

"Lynley, you're not serious about marrying my sister-in-law?"

"What makes you think I'm not serious?" Emily Radstock's overheard outburst was just the stroke of inspiration Lynley needed. Now that he'd been recruited for the spy club, he had been looking for a way to return to society without actually being available to any of the likely candidates for his hand.

"She's...on the shelf...been there for years. You have no pressing reason to marry. Have you?"

"Other than the usual reasons you mean—get an heir, have a ready source of carnal embrace, avoid burning in fiery damnation for all eternity?"

Phil halted abruptly at the corner of David and Grosvenor Streets, his face contracted in puzzlement. The chill wind eddied around them. "No, I was thinking of being in love, of finding another person necessary to your happiness."

"Is that what you did, Phil?" Lynley doubted there was such a thing as one person being necessary to another person's happiness. Happiness itself was perhaps overrated. Besides, what he needed, what he'd discussed only the previous evening with his new employer, Goldsworthy, the spymaster, was a strategy that enabled him to pass among London's fashionable elite, looking for whoever was stealing documents from the Foreign Office and selling them to the Russians.

Phil decided to start walking again. "Couldn't do without Roz."

"And at the time you didn't consider Emily, your sister-in-law? She must have been available." And she was beautiful. Lynley had been gut-punched by her beauty when he'd stood up from behind that flowered monstrosity of a couch. She had nothing of her sister's demure serenity. Her hazel eyes flashed under slashing dark brows, and it had required all his considerable practice in self-containment not to stare at that lush, generous mouth.

Phil shuddered. "Never. She's well-looking, I'm sure, but there's something..."

"Bold, energetic, outspoken about her? Something of a termagant?"

"Yes," said Phil, plainly relieved of the obligation to be tactful about a difficult relation. "She writes letters to the *Times*," he confided.

"Not demure and domestic?"

Phil shook his head. "Not at all."

"That's what I like. She'll do." In truth Lynley had planned to remain hidden and seek the girl out later in a more conventional way, but Phil's entry into the room had forced his hand, and he was not a man to let an opportunity pass.

"Well, that's all right then. I think her parents will be pleased. You'll like the old man."

"I'll call on him today." Lynley clapped his friend on the shoulder. "Shall we see about those horses you're thinking of buying?"

* * * *

Emily clung to the fragile teacup Roz had shoved into her hands as soon as the gentlemen left. A fragrant, reassuring steam wafted up as she tried to think how she had let a man claim her hand when she had set out with only the firm intention of thwarting her mother's management of her life. He could not be serious. He must be making a joke. She didn't like the idea of being a joke. He had not struck her as deficient in understanding, so he must have realized that she didn't really want to marry. "He won't actually put an announcement in the paper."

Roz made no reply.

"He wouldn't dare," Emily said.

Roz shook her head. "I think he'll do just what he says he'll do. He's like that, Em."

"Who is he exactly, and how does he come to be such a friend of Phil's that he can fall asleep on that sofa and you forget he's even there?" Emily stared at the offending sofa. It was another instance of their mother insisting on shaping her children's lives according to her plans. Gentle Roz, now married into a prominent family, was to be a great hostess with a dramatic flair for entertaining. Of course, their mother had tried to take over the decorating of Roz's new townhouse. Roz had simply thanked their mother and gone on with her own scheme of pale blue and gold decoration.

"He's Sir Ajax Lynley. He's a baronet."

"A baronet, the lowest title in the peerage." Emily straightened up. "Well then, whatever Mother thinks, Father will put an end to his pretensions to the hand of an earl's daughter."

"Do you think so?" Roz had taken up the little book and was turning the pages, stopping to let her eyes pass over a passage here and there.

"No, you're right. They will wash their hands of me."

"He is rich, I think."

"Oh, then they really will wash their hands of me." Emily's shoulders slumped again.

"But Em, you said you would marry the first imbecile you met." Roz put the book down and took up her tea.

"But I didn't mean him! I didn't know he was lurking in the shadows behind that wretched sofa, waiting to trap me into marriage."

"He and Phil have been friends forever. Phil consults Lynley whenever he buys horses from a private party. That's what they're doing today, going to look at a pair of...breakdowns, Phil called them."

Emily couldn't hold that against Lynley. She had no objection to a man who knew and appreciated horses.

"Em, you should talk to Mother. Tell her you appreciate her... thoughtfulness in giving you the book, but that you'll find a husband in your own way. I'm sure Lynley will understand if you wish to cry off."

"Will he?"

"You hardly know each other. There's been no courtship. If you make your true feelings known..."

"I'll look like a jilt."

"But you don't care, not much anyway, about others' opinions. You've always said that."

And she wanted to believe it was true, that it didn't matter one jot to her that people thought her a joke or a jilt. She picked up the little book that Roz had put down, and opened it to the preface. The author proposed to help ladies find lasting happiness in marriage through following her guidance. Emily had no objection to happiness, but what if she studied the advice in the little book and then did the opposite? Wouldn't she then force her unexpected suitor to withdraw his suit? Isn't that what Roz had done with their mother? She'd accepted the wretched sofa, and then gone about decorating in the opposite way.

"You know, Roz dear, I think you're right. I should thank Mother and start reading. Who knows what I may discover from this little blue book?"

Chapter Two

The chief task of the husband hunter is one of discernment.
Among the many gentlemen she meets, she seeks one who is
suitable in heart and mind. As she begins her search, she may
imagine that the only man who will suit her is one whose tastes
and ideas exactly match her own, who shares equally in her
likes and dislikes. Indeed, there is a pleasure in discovering
shared tastes and preferences that may blind the husband
hunter to the true nature of the suitability she seeks. A common
taste for Italian opera and the poet Cowper is no basis for
marriage compared with shared principles of integrity and
kindness.

—*The Husband Hunter's Guide to London*

Lynley returned to the spy club by midafternoon. Under the scaffolding and flapping canvas of supposed renovations was the concealed entrance to a fine old building. He supposed that he'd passed the place often enough without giving it a second thought. And he had never guessed there was an entrance through a fashionable chemist's shop around the corner.

Nate Wilde, the youth Lynley had abducted while playing highwayman—or rescued, really, from the traitor Radcliffe's trigger-happy stagecoach guards—was there to greet him and take his hat and coat. Wilde still had his arm in a sling, but cheerfully managed his duties as the club's major domo with assistance from the beautiful daughter of the spies' tailor.

"Coffee, sir?"

Lynley nodded. He found the club to his liking. He could stroll into the quiet, well-appointed coffee room at any hour of the day or night and find a degree of comfort and privacy not readily available even in some of the finest houses. He liked the simplicity of the room with its velvet curtains and high white ceiling, and its substantial but plain mantel, nothing ornate, and no paintings of saints or martyrs. A man could think his own thoughts here without interference or rebuke. He sank down on one of the room's long couches, shed his boots and settled himself, his feet toward the fire. He did his best thinking lying down, and he had some thinking to do about his strategy for approaching Lady Emily Radstock's father, Lord Candover.

If Lynley had any complaint to make about the club, it was that as yet he had done no spying. But that would change tonight, if the afternoon's interviews went successfully. His betrothal would provide the cover story his employer demanded.

According to the briefing he'd received from Goldsworthy, the club spymaster, a spy was loose in London society, who had in his or her possession, letters of the most sensitive nature between the Persian shah and his son and chief commander, at the very moment when a misstep in sensitive negotiations taking place in the East could plunge England into a war in defense of Persia.

Lynley was to be the newest weapon in the war the Foreign Office waged at home against those who would betray English secrets to Russian agents. Whoever had acquired the shah's papers would be eager to get them into Russian hands for a profit, and the old way of doing so through Sir Geoffrey Radcliffe's stagecoach line had now ended. So the man or woman with the papers must be desperate.

Lynley was impatient to begin the work. He had managed to extract some useful information about Emily Radstock's family from Phil while they considered the merits of a pair of horses that Mudford wanted to sell. Like most men of fashion, Mudford bought his horses for their showy appearance, and then blamed them for equine vices more likely due to mishandling than to flaws in their temperament. In promoting Phil's purchase, Lynley would be doing the horses a favor.

Wilde returned with the coffee and stirred the fire to crackling life. Lynley sat up and poured himself a generous cup. One thing Phil had mentioned stuck in his brain. Emily Radstock had written letters to the *Times.*

"Wilde, do you have any recent issues of the *Times*?"

"Of course, sir. Shall I collect them for you?"

When Lynley nodded, the youth disappeared to find the club's copies of the *Times,* Lynley had no doubt. Lynley wanted to see one of those letters. Phil's information did not quite explain how a beautiful young woman from a well-connected aristocratic family had reached the age of twenty-eight, almost -nine, without marrying, especially when there was nothing in Emily's appearance or her father's bank account to put off potential suitors. Lynley had gathered from the overheard conversation with her sister, that Emily was of an outspoken and independent nature, but he did not detect vanity or petulance, the usual defects of character to which a striking beauty might be prey.

Lynley thought he could persuade her father to agree to the match. Though his title was undistinguished, his fortune was large. His estate at Lyndale Abbey was a decent property. Furthermore, if he read the situation right, Lady Emily's mother at least believed her daughter had diminished prospects for marriage at her age, and therefore a pair of shrewd parents might not question his sudden suit too closely.

Persuading Emily herself that their betrothal, however sudden and of whatever duration they chose to make it, was to her advantage—that was the challenge. He knew nothing of her experience with men, but he guessed that something a man had done made Emily Radstock resolve to accept the first "imbecile" she met.

Phil seemed to think that there had been an attachment to which the family had objected. In any case, Lynley needed to act. His sense of Emily Radstock told him that she did not like to be vulnerable, and he didn't want to give her any time to arm herself against him. He had a ring that would serve his purpose, and a card of invitation procured by Goldsworthy to a gathering that could prove a good spy-hunting ground.

If he could get his ring on Emily Radstock's finger, he could begin tonight.

* * * *

The second time Emily Radstock met Ajax Lynley was no less unsettling than the first. In her mother's rather passé Egyptian drawing room, his height and ease of manner gave Emily a sense of an adult invading the nursery, towering over the child-sized furnishings, hobbyhorses, and toy houses. The sheer size of him stopped her brain for a moment. Emily never felt small. She was no Cinderella whose tiny foot captured a prince. She had her father's feet, and fit as comfortably in his shoes as in her own.

She offered tea, which Lynley declined. He did not look any less sure of himself, but she would give him a way out in case he'd done some thinking over the intervening hours. She had read three chapters of the little book since their last meeting, but when he'd been announced, she'd had only a few minutes to apply its principles in reverse.

"I trust you've thought the better of your...idea since this morning."

"Not at all," he said with grating good cheer.

She wished he would sit. He was not perfectly handsome. If one looked closely, one saw a flaw in his mouth, a quirk in his upper lip on the left side, so his lips did not close completely. A thin thread of a white scar slanted across the place.

"What could you possibly mean by accepting me? You are not, I presume, an imbecile?"

He shook his head. "No one has ever accused me of lacking intelligence. I will follow your lead in setting a date for our nuptials. But we need a story to tell the world—how we met and wooed, fell in love and plighted our troth."

"We could say that you eavesdropped on a private conversation and took advantage of an unguarded remark."

He went on as if he hadn't heard her. "If you are an advocate for truthfulness, we can say that we met through your sister and Phil. Your visits to support your sister as she prepares for the birth of her child, and my visits to consult with Phil about the purchase of a new pair of horses, inevitably threw us together. And love"—he made a brief circle in the air with one lean, strong hand—"ensued."

"Ensued?" Emily fell back against the couch cushions, lifting a hand to her brow. "Oh, the romance of it all! I don't know whether to take up my fan or my smelling salts."

He leaned one elbow on the low mantel. It wasn't low at all except to him. "Ah, it is, I fear, all too common a story, is it not? Lovers meeting in the midst of their families, left alone because no one imagines such a meeting has the power to stir the soul?"

"You don't write fiction, do you?" Emily asked, straightening back up.

"No." He sat down opposite her. "You would prefer a more romantic story? I could figure as a dashing hero who swept in to rescue you from some peril—coaching accident on an icy road? Footpads outside the theater? Wild bull in a field?—and within moments of our meeting we discovered how ardently we both admire the same poets."

"I beg to differ with you. You do write fiction."

He regarded her narrowly. "You've done something to yourself since this morning."

She could not repress a smile. "I've been reading my husband-hunting guide." She batted her lashes at him. It was more difficult than she had imagined.

He stood and crossed the room, reaching down and taking her chin in one hand and producing a handkerchief in the other hand. "Do you have something in your eye?" he asked.

Emily snatched the handkerchief and pressed it to the side of her face. Did he not understand the most basic weapon in the arsenal of the flirt? Against her skin the square of linen was crisp and clean and smelled of sage and cardamom and him. She handed it back. "Thank you."

"It's your hair," he said, frowning. "I thought our betrothal saved you from enslaving yourself to that book."

Emily sighed. "You cannot blame me for being uncertain as to the genuineness of your intentions or for wanting to do all in my power to secure...happiness in marriage."

He reached in a pocket of his waistcoat and produced a ring.

Emily stared. Lying in his palm was a large, square amethyst set in gold surrounded by tiny diamonds—well, not so tiny. Each was the size of a respectable grain of sand. Such a ring was not a joke. Her throat felt too dry for speech.

"It's not customary," he said, "but I think it will suit you, you know."

Emily looked up at him. She had been sure not two minutes earlier that he was teasing her and treating his proposal as a joke. Now she did not know how to read him. Reason said he was not a man in love, but he was plainly in earnest about their engagement.

She could take the ring. She could let it flash and dazzle on her finger as she made her way through the Season her mother wanted her to have, but she had to remember that no matter the beauty of the gem, his rash suit could not be motivated by love. He could not want her. She had to hold on to that idea as firmly and resolutely as she had ever held on to her understanding of gravity. Failing to grasp that one could not walk on air could be fatal.

She extended her left hand. He took it, letting it rest in his larger hand a moment. Then he slid the ring down her finger, and she lifted her hand from his. She caught a look of relief in his eyes at her acceptance.

"Tonight, then?" he said.

"Tonight?" She looked up at him.

"A supper and dancing at Lady Ravenhurst's."

"My father's cousin?"

"I hear she gives a good supper."

She nodded. Whatever else the Season now held, it was her chance to figure out what he really was up to.

* * * *

Emily sat down to review her strategy. She kicked off her shoes and swung her feet up onto a nile-green striped sofa from Mama's early Egyptian phase and stretched out her hand. The diamonds on her finger winked up at her with all the deep concern of distant stars for the doings of men. Her first attempt to put off Ajax Lynley had only landed her deeper in the briars.

She tried not to think about the conversation happening in her father's library between her betrothed and her about-to-be-quite-surprised father. Papa liked order and sameness, not surprises.

If she examined her feelings at the moment, she had to admit that the low spirits she usually felt at the prospect of an evening among the fashionable elite of London had evaporated.

The prospect of a Season as an engaged woman intrigued her. The bold ring on her finger wiped away past Seasons of failure. She would not be an object of pitying looks. No one would shun her lest the awkwardness of her situation prove catching. People would wonder, of course, how she, of all wallflowers, could have managed to snare such an eligible man.

How to enjoy confounding the doubters while working to free herself from the baronet was the dilemma. Her first effort of overcomplicating her hair with ringlets and braids had hardly slowed him down at all. He had noticed the change and gone ahead with his plan to announce their engagement, just as if she had not resembled Medusa on a bad day. Apparently, he did not require beauty in a wife.

She had got so far in her thinking when the drawing room door burst open and her papa strode in. He had a handsome, affable face warmed by a full head of golden brown hair and smile lines around his eyes, but he could frown, and when he did, what one noticed were his stiff bearing and slashing dark brows. Emily swung her feet to the floor and stood up.

"Girl, what have you done?"

"Why, got engaged, Papa. Nothing remarkable in that."

"After five years of resisting and avoiding suitors, you chose today to give in?"

"Mama encouraged me to go forward." Emily resisted the desire to curl her bare toes into the carpet.

Her father's passion was building projects, and his guiding principle in life was to keep her mother happy. If that meant Egyptian furnishings in the drawing room or charitable contributions to various ladies' organizations, he provided. He rarely took note of his children's doings, except when his wife's happiness might be disturbed, or when one of Emily's letters reached the *Times*.

"When?" Papa looked skeptical.

"This morning."

"He's a better choice than your first attempt at it, I'll give you that."

She had to agree. Her first love had flattered her and flirted shamelessly while secretly pursuing a different heiress. She had been completely taken in. "You gave him your consent then?"

"I did. You'll not get out of it that way."

"I just got in, Papa." Emily held out her ring for him to admire.

He glanced at it. "You waited for your mother to be away."

Emily shrugged. "I could hardly help Grandmother's being ill."

"Well, this Lynley fellow appears to know his mind. He's off to put an announcement in the papers."

"I'll send an express to Mama directly."

"Where did you meet him?"

"Did he not tell you? At Roz's house. He likes horses, you know."

"Whatever you've done to your hair, your mother would not like it." The parent who rarely paid attention to her appeared uncomfortably penetrating at the moment.

"Yes, Papa."

"I suppose your mother will want to give a party." He was losing interest, turning another domestic matter over to the women in his life.

"Time enough to worry about parties when Mama returns."

* * * *

On his return to the club, Lynley received an order, transmitted by Wilde, to report to the spies' tailor, Kirby. He supposed that at some future time he would dislike orders, but for now he was enjoying the workings of the spy club.

Wilde handed him the stack of newspapers he'd requested, and tucking the papers under his arm, Lynley made his way out through the kitchen and across the little yard separating the club from the chemist's shop that housed the tailor's fitting room. Spying and tailoring both depended for their success on attention to detail, and Kirby, whose shop dealt in soaps, lotions, and powders as a cover, was a master at the trade.

In between measurings and fittings for suitable black evening wear, Lynley lounged on a rug-padded bench and worked his way through the pile of newspapers, looking for letters from his betrothed. He had just found a letter signed *E. Radstock* when he became aware of a shadow cast over the page. He glanced up to find Goldsworthy looming over him.

"Well, lad, have you got your cover settled? Are you ready to make a start?"

With a greatcoat over his massive bulk, Goldsworthy blocked the light from the back room's high window. Lynley folded the page of the *Times,* and endeavoring to maintain an offhand air, jammed it into a pocket. He looked up at his new commander. "I'll be taking Lady Emily to the Ravenhursts' tonight. Anything more I should know?"

Goldsworthy gave him little space, but Lynley managed to stand. He had stood for every scold of his life, never permitting either his diminutive aunt or his willowy uncle to stand over him. He liked meeting an opponent eye to eye, and Goldsworthy was an opponent of sorts, always testing one's mettle.

"Lord Candover's daughter has agreed to the match?"

"She has."

"Excellent. There's no better cover than playing the besotted swain to some chit for the Season. Had Blackstone do it. Worked a charm. Now then..." Goldsworthy turned to the cutting table and slapped down a rolled-up paper. "The sooner you can smoke this fellow out, the better."

Kirby gave a polite cough. "If we could finish Sir Ajax's coat first, Mr. G."

"Of course, of course." The big man waved a hand for Kirby to continue, and Kirby motioned Lynley to try on a black evening coat with long tails.

By *fellow*, Goldsworthy meant the person who was holding on to a group of letters between the ruler of Persia and his son Prince Mirza, translated into English by Willock, the English chargé d'affaires who kept his own extensive network of spies in the Persian court. In Russian hands those letters could ensnare England in a foreign war.

It had been some time since Lynley had thought of Russia as his enemy. That thinking belonged to a foolish boy unable to distinguish between the one man who had injured him, and a whole nation. Still, the case revived the old enmity he'd felt against his mother's lover.

Just weeks earlier the club's former spies, Hazelwood and Clare, had managed to snare the Russian Count Malikov with incriminating documents in his possession. Malikov, who wasn't talking, now languished in a cell pending the outcome of negotiations between his government and England's. The English were quite willing to let the count rot there until Lynley could find Malikov's source.

Several links in the chain forged by Malikov to convey documents from Lord Chartwell's office to St. Petersburg were broken, but somewhere in London was that cache of leaked letters.

Part of the puzzle was how such an extensive collection of papers had gone missing. Goldsworthy reasoned that whoever had the letters must be eager to get them to the Russians, who paid well for information, and very uneasy about being found with the incriminating documents. Suspicion had turned, fairly or unfairly, to Lady Ravenhurst's husband, a devoted Foreign Office drudge, as the source of the leak. In the weeks before his arrest, Malikov had often been a guest of Lady Ravenhurst's. Goldsworthy was keen to show Lynley the layout of the lady's house.

When Kirby released Lynley from the fitting, promising to have the coat ready for the evening, Goldsworthy unrolled a floor plan of the Ravenhurst house on the tailor's cutting table. "Usually, we'd put Wilde on the staff, to help you out, but with the boy's arm in a sling, we can't use him for a week or so. You'll be working alone tonight."

Working alone suited Lynley just fine. He studied the floor plan. The house was grander than most London row houses, with five windows across the front, but it was easy to see how the position of the stairs and doors made Ravenhurst's library vulnerable from the entry hall and the grand dining room.

Lynley pictured the guests moving through the evening ahead, from the arrival and greeting, to the supper that would confine them to the dining room for hours, through the traditional interlude of separation between the ladies and gentlemen after the meal, and finally to the dancing. Somehow in between the rituals that punctuated the flow of a London evening, he would have to search the house. The trick for Lynley would be to make himself invisible to his hosts and fellow guests long enough to determine how someone might have stolen the documents.

Goldsworthy rolled up the house plan and gave Lynley a clap on the back like a cricket bat connecting with a ball. "Good to have you on the case, lad."

Lynley shook off the big man's hearty approval and returned to the coffee room and his favorite sofa. As he sank into its comfort, the copy of the *Times* rustled under him. He pulled it out, drew a lamp near, and began to read. Emily Radstock had written concerning the recent death of the elephant Chunee at the hands of his caretakers.

Sir:

The facts in the death of Chunee are so well known as to need no recounting. Thousands in London have seen the prints depicting his cruel slaughter. His agony at the hands of those on whom he long depended for his sustenance and whose pockets were lined with the proceeds of exhibiting him to the public is indefensible.

His handlers' inability to consider his needs and to foresee a time when distress of body and spirit would render him a danger to himself and others and to plan accordingly for his care and ultimately for his end brings into question the fitness of human persons for keeping any wild animals in captivity, confined against their nature in cages, to be stared at by the masses with no freedom to act in accord with the promptings of their natures.

It is time to close the Exeter Change and all similar institutions whose indifference to the well-being of their charges is a stain on the honor of our city.

I am, Sir, your obedient servant,
E. Radstock

Every sentence rang with fierce conviction and independence of mind. He admired her stand against cruelty. But it was her contempt for the betrayal at the heart of the elephant's suffering that made him shake his head as he folded the paper and tucked it back into his coat. She spoke of agony, but what, after all, did she know of the pain of betrayal?

He recognized her spirit though. She was the sort who thought the world could be a better place, who believed in noble sacrifice, who thought she could make a difference. As a girl she had probably nursed butterflies and kept hurt birds in boxes in her room. To care about caged elephants and the weak and the vulnerable was to risk great heartache.

He would wager the price of a good horse that she knew nothing about having fun. Few people knew how genuinely to enjoy themselves. They were always doing their duty. As for saving the world, or even saving England, that was for other fellows. He needed an adventure, and if the British government wanted to house and feed and clothe him while he had his adventure, and compensate him for it in the end, he was fine with that.

And along the way, he might teach Lady Emily Radstock what it meant to have fun.

Chapter Three

The husband hunter may expect the announcement of her betrothal to be met with surprise, curiosity, and even genuine delight. What she must not expect is that such an announcement will be met with tact. Whether the news bursts upon her acquaintance at a ball, whether it is the whispered gossip of a morning call, or whether her neighbors and friends see the printed notice in the paper, everyone acquainted with either party will have an opinion as to how deserving each is of the other, and few will resist the temptation to comment.

—The Husband Hunter's Guide to London

Within a few moments of entering Ravenhurst House, Lynley had a fair idea of how carelessly his host and hostess ran their household. Unconventionally, Lady Ravenhurst mingled with her guests in the marble entry chamber. Servants rushed from guest to guest, collecting coats and hats and pointing the way to the stairs. It was the sort of din and confusion in which pickpockets thrived in marketplaces all over the world.

Lady Ravenhurst fit Goldsworthy's report of her. She was a deep-breasted golden beauty, who appeared to be of a restless, impatient disposition. Seven years into her marriage to Ravenhurst, she had a reputation as a dashing hostess. Her laugh had a brittle edge as she flirted with a pair of younger gentlemen.

Lynley turned from his hostess to make note of servants passing in and out of an open closet in front of him and the entrance to Ravenhurst's library opposite the grand stairway. As he slipped Lady Emily's black satin cloak from her shoulders, he thought he'd fumbled the simple gesture. Her outer garment fell away, and she appeared dressed in a shroud of deep ebony. Very little of her person was visible.

She turned to him with a guileless smile. He handed her cloak to the waiting footman, making no sign of anything out of the ordinary in her dress, as if going to a fashionable dinner with a woman dressed like a hearse horse was an ordinary occurrence. Clearly, his betrothed was up to something.

He offered his arm, and her touch sent a current of sensation through him. How carefully she'd planned her surprise. She had been cloaked and ready to meet him at her father's door, and she'd kept her hair simple. Nothing in her outward appearance had prepared him for what she'd been hiding under that cloak. He led her toward the stairs.

"It is customary for a gentleman to offer a lady some compliment on her attire," she said.

"Is it? I must be out of practice." He resisted the kick in his pulse at the thought that she had been thinking of him as she dressed, standing before her glass in a shift and corset. She was testing him, daring him to react, inviting him to play a game.

They passed from the top of the stairs into a great room already set up for dancing with the rugs removed and the furnishings pushed to the perimeter. Lynley noted a small dais at the far end with chairs for musicians and a potted palm at the edge that concealed what might be a useful door.

Their host, Ravenhurst, stood to one side in conversation with Lord Chartwell of the Foreign Office. Ravenhurst gave only a distracted greeting as guests entered, returning at once to his conversation with Chartwell. As Emily and Lynley passed the two men, Lynley caught the words of an impassioned assurance from Ravenhurst to Chartwell. "We'll get him tonight. I promise you."

Chartwell made only a brief, close-lipped reply. "If he takes the bait, Ravenhurst."

"He will."

"He'd better."

Chartwell moved off, and Lynley glanced round to see whether anyone else noted the exchange.

Lynley's mouth tightened. It was not a house where vital documents would be safe.

* * * *

An hour spent among the Ravenhursts' guests did not alter Lynley's opinion. As the guests descended for supper, many passed through the open doors of the library before realizing their mistake. Some guests turned back, blocking the smooth flow to the dining room.

Lord Ravenhurst took charge, assuring his confused guests that they could pass through the library into the dining room. Lynley steered Emily Radstock that way.

Before the window stood a mahogany desk with a red leather government documents box in plain sight and a number of papers lying on the desk's surface around it. Lynley's path through the library did not permit him to observe the papers closely, but he suspected that at least one of them had to be the bait Ravenhurst had mentioned to Chartwell, a paper that would be marked as a Foreign Office "confidential print."

In spite of the confusion on entering the dining room, the guests were seated in minutes. From the head of the table Ravenhurst looked directly toward his library. Then Lady Ravenhurst signaled her butler to close the doors, and the footmen began to serve. Lynley set himself to observe his fellow guests and wait for one of them to make a move toward the door, though he thought it unlikely that a clever spy would fall for Ravenhurst's bait.

Two hours later Lynley discovered how wrong he was. Servants moved in and out of the dining room as the gentlemen lingered over a good port and a weak sherry. Ravenhurst made a point of bringing the conversation around to the importance of the papers he handled for the Foreign Office. Lynley left the dining room with a pair of gentlemen intent on smoking outside. Another brief ruse and he was on his own. For the moment no one occupied the library, and by standing to one side of the dining room door, Lynley could look at Ravenhurst's desk unobserved from either the hall or the dining room. The papers had been moved. The thief had been quick and had settled for one paper at best.

When he heard Ravenhurst coming, Lynley backed into the entry and slipped into the darkened cloakroom. It occurred to him as he stood among the coats and cloaks that a clever thief might slip a stolen paper into a pocket or a sleeve for later retrieval.

* * * *

Emily was waltzing with Ajax Lynley when the full force of her folly hit her. She had dressed to test his resolve as a suitor. Her gown was the oldest one she could find in her mother's closet, a black crape with a high, tight bodice ten years out of fashion and long, loose sleeves that bore a strong resemblance to elephant trunks.

She had counted on shocking him, but if he had recognized her attire as a crime against fashion, he gave no sign of it. Now, she could only look at him as they whirled around the room, for if she allowed her gaze to wander she would encounter the glances of the curious and the judgmental.

After her disastrous third Season when she had tried in earnest to find a husband, she had confined herself to the margins of fashionable gatherings. Now, with an announcement in the papers, a ring on her finger, and the substantial person of Sir Ajax Lynley at her side, she had been lured from the shadows into the glare of public notice.

They were noticed. He, at any rate, was impossible to overlook in a ballroom. His height, his dark good looks, his assured manner drew glances. He appeared oblivious to whispers and stares. And yet, twice in the evening he had vanished from her sight, and she had no idea how he'd contrived to do it or where he'd disappeared.

He plainly knew his way around a ballroom, but she did not remember him from any previous Season.

"Where were you?" she asked.

"When?" He lifted his heavy-lidded gaze, and she realized he'd been looking at her bosom, what little of it her mother's gown exposed.

"These last few Seasons?"

"In Spain."

"The war ended years ago."

"My uncle has business there."

Emily gave him a sharp glance. His reply told her nothing really. She tried a different tack. "How do you bear being looked at so much?"

A hint of amusement lightened his gaze. "Do you think anyone sees us? Really sees us?"

"What do you think they see?"

One of his black brows lifted. "Clothes. I'm sure there are women in this room who can name your...mother's modiste, and gentlemen who'd like to know the name of my tailor."

Emily could not help the laugh that escaped her. So he had noticed her gown after all.

He pulled her a fraction closer, settling her more firmly in his hold as the tempo of the dance accelerated. The plan was to keep him at a distance until she understood him better. She had not counted on the intimacy of the waltz. Or the dizzying effect of being held so closely. He smelled of citrus and cardamom and woods and smoke.

She had endured enough awkward partners in her first three Seasons to marvel a little at how easily they moved together. For a few moments she was caught up in admiring the way he communicated how they would move together. A light touch, the pressure of his hand, the tilt of his head invited her partnership in the dance. It seemed a miracle that he heard the beat as she did. It made her more curious to know his past.

"Why did you return?" she asked as the dance ended and he tucked her arm in his.

"I inherited." He whispered it in her ear as if he were confiding a lover's secret. "Something to drink?" he asked. She nodded, and he slipped away. Like that the intimacy of their dance dissolved. She could see only the back of his head above the crowd as he disappeared through the doors to the refreshment room.

She turned back to find a lady in a fashionable gown of lemon-colored Turkish satin.

"Emily Radstock," said the vision in yellow, "whatever are you wearing?"

"I'm in mourning for Chunee." Emily said the first thing that came to mind, referring to the poor elephant brutally killed at the Exeter Change.

The lady in yellow laughed, and Emily remembered her name. *Miss Sophia Throckmorton.* They'd been introduced at a party not a fortnight earlier. The girl was just what a husband hunter ought to be, as bright and shiny as a new-minted coin.

"Oh, I'm glad you explained," she said. "It's so common for ladies who don't take simply to give up on fashion." Miss Throckmorton's fan waved gently just below her magnificent bosom. "Of course, now that you have a fiancé, perhaps you are no longer a slave to appearance as we younger ladies are."

A pair of ladies laughed at that and joined them. Kitty Beckford and her sister Clarissa. Emily made the introductions.

"Oh, Emily, I heard the news," Kitty said. "I never imagined you would have to wait so long to find a husband."

"Obscure title," Miss Throckmorton observed, "but at your time of life, one does what one must. Where is he, by the way? You'd think he would be eager to be at your side every minute."

"At least he's very rich," Emily said.

When Lynley did not return with the promised refreshment, his absence began to look like abandonment, or like repaying her for dressing as she had. He had whirled her about the dance floor for everyone to see, and then left her to face the consequences of her choices in fashion and fiancés.

As long as he had been at her side, her black gown had not set her so wholly apart from the other women, but on her own, she looked like a crow at a dove party. She had tried to discompose him with the gown. Instead she had driven him away. She would have to think of a better way to knock him off balance. At the moment what she wanted was escape.

When Miss Throckmorton moved on to her next victim, Emily stepped back from the little group of ladies and edged her way toward a large potted palm at the end of the musicians' dais and slipped behind it. There she came face-to-face with one of the fiddlers, who gave her a wink and a leer, and mouthed a *hello* that sent a wave of spirits over her. She stepped back and collided with a door handle. She reached behind her, pulled it, and slipped into the dark space between the inner and outer doors of the ballroom.

The door closed behind her, cutting off the music and gaiety of the dancing. At once she knew she was not alone. A large gloved hand covered her mouth, and a strong arm seized her by the waist. Her heart pounded in her chest. She pulled at the hand covering her mouth, but could not budge it. A voice in her ear whispered, "Quiet, my love." Simultaneously, her senses recognized him, his height, and the bracing blend of citrus and smoke that was *Lynley*.

Emily eased her grip on his arm. *Why is he hiding?*

At once two voices could be heard on the other side of the door. He was eavesdropping. Emily recognized the voices—Lord and Lady Ravenhurst.

"Don't be absurd," the lady was saying. "We can't search our guests. We'll insult everyone. We'll be the laughingstock of London."

"Pamela, you'll ruin me. You don't understand what's at stake."

"So you've told me a hundred times, Ravenhurst. Matters of state are too subtle for my female brain. But it's you who fails to understand anything."

"You can't wish another war on England."

"War? Hah! You think the papers in one of your little red boxes could cause a war? You're mad as well as absurd."

"Just don't try to stop me, wife. Every guest must be searched. I've instructed the footmen. They know what to do."

"How dare you? I must speak to them immediately. I refuse to let you embarrass me before our friends."

"Pamela, I warn you. Obey me in this matter, or I won't pay your gaming debts."

There came a gasp, a ringing slap, and swift footsteps retreating. Emily didn't move. She was pressed tight against Lynley's body in the dark. He was perfectly still, alert, waiting.

At last a second set of heavier footsteps moved away. Lynley's tension eased. He turned her toward him in the dark as the footsteps descended the stairs. She had thought little until now of the space between doors. It was an architectural quirk of grand London houses, these pockets of darkness the thickness of the wall's stone blocks between the inner and outer doors of grand rooms. She had passed through them hundreds of times without a thought.

"Awkward, isn't it?" he said. "To catch a glimpse backstage of our hosts' unhappiness."

"We could hardly help it, could we?" He'd gotten her into this. If he hadn't left her, she would have stayed in the ballroom. She had not deliberately set out to listen to a private conversation. She tilted her face up. She could see nothing of Lynley in the dark, but she sensed he was amused. His flawed mouth would be smiling, exposing that gap between his lips.

"Handy space for escaping, isn't it?" he said.

Maybe she had misjudged him. Maybe Lynley did not like being stared at any more than Chunee had. "Is that what you were up to?"

"It certainly is what you were doing." His hands moved up from her waist to cup her shoulders and pull her closer against him. Her head fit just under his jaw, her ear pressed to the white linen at his throat. For a moment she seemed to breathe him in.

"After you left me at the mercy of London's most cutthroat husband hunters."

"Were they hard on your black gown?"

She nodded against his chest and his arms tightened around her. "And on my engagement at such an advanced old age to a man with an obscure title."

"Ouch. Did you defend me at all?"

"I said that you are very rich."

"Good for you."

"Are you going to tell me what you are really doing, hiding in here?"

One of his hands moved languidly down her spine. "Besides waiting for you to find me where we might be alone?"

"Yes, besides that."

The hand moved up again. "Hmmm. Are you going to tell me why you chose your mother's black gown?"

"A woman wants to know that a man appreciates more than her...beauty."

"Her wit, for instance?" The hand on her back kept up its lazy drift. Her thoughts narrowed to the path of his fingers along her spine. The movement of his hand seemed almost idle, without intention, and yet her pulse began to race and in a confused moment she pressed more closely against him, as if seeking something from his solid bulk.

She started to pull back, when his hands captured her head and tilted her face up to his, and his mouth came down on hers in the dark. The kiss held her suspended weightless as air, neither breathing nor moving, caught in a swift upward flight of exhilaration. Then, as they had in the dance, they plunged together deeper into the kiss.

Emily could not say how long it went on, or how it ended. His arms were tight around her. He felt as solid and immovable as stone, while she was light-headed and giddy.

"Can you help me?" he was saying.

"What?" Emily tried to yank her wayward thoughts back to the moment. She was lurking in a closet, or nearly a closet, the sort of place where a footman might sneak to steal a kiss from a housemaid.

"I think it's time to restore marital harmony to the house. Will you help me?" he asked.

He meant Lord and Lady Ravenhurst. Emily thought marital harmony unlikely between the pair they had overheard. "What do you mean to do?"

"We've got to stop the search. Will you help me create a distraction?"

We? How had they *become* we? "How?"

"Can you drop something over the balustrade?"

"Like what?" He still had his arms around her, but it was clear that his mind was somewhere else.

"Something that will need to be mopped up."

"You're serious."

"Give me ten minutes. Are you willing?"

"Yes," her kiss-disordered brain answered.

He cracked open the door to the hall. A sliver of light exposed the black of his evening clothes and the bright gleam of adventure in his eye. Then he was gone, and Emily heard his footsteps on the stairs. He was leaving it to her, trusting her to act.

She slipped back into the ballroom behind the potted palm. The leering fiddler, in the midst of a lively country-dance, did not notice her. Emily moved easily along the edge of the room, looking for something to drop over the balustrade.

She saw just the thing when a harried-looking footman set a tray on one of the side tables and began loading it with empty drinks glasses. While his back was turned, Emily snagged the tray, turned away, and headed for the open doors of the ballroom.

She stepped to the edge of the balustrade and peered down at the expanse of marble floor below her. Once again the angry voices of her host and hostess filled the air. Emily held out the tray, and let it go. For a moment she thought she'd gone mad. The silver tray and the glassware separated in air into a noiseless glittering stream. Emily held her breath. Then tray and glass shattered against the marble floor below with an appalling splintering, jangling noise that echoed off stone, the noise of things breaking that could never be put together again. A terrible silence followed. Emily stepped away from the balustrade.

Chapter Four

Nothing the husband hunter encounters in the Season is as potentially misleading as a kiss. It is wise to avoid as much as possible those locales, which favor such expressions of feeling. The very circumstances in which the husband hunter is likely to succumb to the promptings of her heart or the persuasions of a gentleman, if such a man may retain the title, do not make for clear thinking. Moonlit gardens, dark balconies, and fireworks displays by their very nature obscure sight.

—*The Husband Hunter's Guide to London*

Lynley silently applauded Emily's resourcefulness as he stepped from the library into the entry hall. The shattering glass had just the desired effect. His own head, still muddled by the kiss in the closet, cleared, and the Ravenhursts' servants came running. Brooms and dustpans were fetched, and the work of sweeping up the glass, tiny fragments of which glittered from one end of the hall to the other, began. No one noted the odd direction of his entry on the scene.

Ravenhurst and his lady stood watching in silence. Ravenhurst saw Lynley first.

"Lynley, what are you doing here?"

Lynley lifted the coat draped over his arm. "Came to collect my coat and say goodnight, old man. Couldn't help but overhear. Are you missing something?"

Lady Ravenhurst gave a dry laugh. "His wits."

"Vital Foreign Office papers, if you must know," Ravenhurst snarled.

"Where should we look?"

Ravenhurst tightened his jaw. "Someone's taken them. I'll have everyone searched."

Lynley held his arms out and assumed an expression he hoped would pass for imbecilic. "Well, you can start with me, old man, but I often find the thing I'm looking for in some place I've forgotten. Shall we search your library?"

"Do," said Lady Ravenhurst. "Take my absurd husband away to his precious library."

"You know, Ravenhurst," Lynley said, "we really should talk about your cellar."

"My cellar?"

"The sherry's execrable."

Ravenhurst shot his wife one last glare, then stalked to the library. Lynley trailed after him.

* * * *

Emily hurried down the stairs. On the strength of a kiss in a closet she had done something outrageous. Ever since Lynley had raised his head above that wretched sofa in Rosalind's drawing room, she'd been off balance. She needed to regain her senses. She could hear footmen talking, the tinkle of glass fragments being swept up, and the rumble of Lynley's voice in conversation with their hosts.

As she turned to descend the final run of stairs, a footman held up a hand to stop her. "Best to wait, miss. Broken glass about."

From below Lady Ravenhurst looked up and shuddered as her gaze took in Emily's black gown.

"Sorry to disturb," Emily murmured. Her black gown, which had seemed a good joke at the start of the evening, now appeared to be a piece of utter folly. "I'm looking for Lynley. We were about to leave."

"He's in the library with my husband."

"Oh."

Lady Ravenhurst appeared lost, her violet eyes staring blankly, her hands hanging limp at her sides. She was one of those females Emily could never be—the helpless and fragile kind that compelled men to rush to their sides offering all manner of assistance. From above came the music and laughter of the ballroom. It was hard to stand saying nothing, offering no comfort to the woman before her, not knowing what exactly was wrong, but Emily knew it was what she must do, until the footmen withdrew.

When they did, she came down the steps, trying to think of what to say beyond the inadequate commonplaces of leave-taking. She could hear Lynley's voice from within the library and ventured a thank-you. She added, "Tonight Lynley and I enjoyed our first waltz."

Lady Ravenhurst's gaze returned to Emily's gown. "Betrothed, are you? How fitting that you wore black. I can't imagine a worse fate for a woman than gaining a husband." She turned away but stopped as Ravenhurst and Lynley emerged from the library.

"No need to search the guests, after all, Pamela," Lord Ravenhurst declared. The anger had gone out of his voice, replaced by a puzzled tone. He shrugged. "Lynley found the missing papers."

Lady Ravenhurst started and directed a searching look at Lynley. "Thank you." She recovered some of her composure. "I did not care to have our guests treated like common thieves."

"Of course, Lady Ravenhurst. Easiest thing in the world for papers to get out of order. Mine do so all the time," Lynley assured them affably.

Emily watched her fiancé. His expression was cheerfully blank, as if he did not see his hosts' misery. She recalled his words in the dark about seeing backstage at the play. What they had overheard together was only part of the story. The other part was a mystery. To Emily his disappearances over the course of the evening now appeared connected, and missing papers, not a broken marriage, seemed to be the heart of the matter.

"Lady Emily?" He crossed the hall and extended a hand to her. "Shall we take our leave?"

Without apparent hurry, he wrapped Emily in her cloak and led her out to their waiting carriage. His servant leaped to open the door and let down the step. Lynley helped her inside, tucked a rug over her skirts, and stepped away. He held the carriage door open with his back, watching her, making no move to enter.

"Lynley," she said, "are you going to tell me what you were really doing at that party?"

"Dancing with my betrothed, sharing our happy news with the world."

Emily shook her head. "You managed the return of those missing papers. Why? Not out of a deep concern for the state of the Ravenhursts' marriage."

"Anyone who knows them must be concerned," he said. "I must take my leave of you."

"What? Am I missing something?"

"Yes. This," he said. He pulled her forward to the edge of the seat and kissed her with an almost ruthless fierceness. He pulled back, and Emily tried to recover her breath and wits.

"Changes everything, don't you see?" He shut the carriage door and signaled the coachman to drive, and Emily fell back on the seat, her senses in a flurry, her thoughts in turmoil.

* * * *

Lynley returned to the club near three. He handed his hat and coat to a yawning Wilde, who relayed Goldsworthy's request for a report.

"Does he ever sleep?" Lynley looked at the beckoning couches of the coffee room.

Wilde shook his head. "He had a message from Chartwell at midnight, sir. Woke him right up."

With a last look at his favorite couch, Lynley headed up the stairs to Goldsworthy's office.

Inside the big man's lair, the air was cold and the lamps, dim. A desk the size of a Thames barge dominated the room with a pair of green leather chairs facing it like bits of flotsam floating in the great barge's wake. Canvas from the supposed renovation project draped two of the walls. A third was covered in maps of London and the surrounding country. The last was lined with cabinets of various sizes and many drawers.

"Lad, what news?"

Lynley had a fleeting thought that the drawers contained information the spymaster was reluctant to share. He took one of the chairs opposite and had the satisfaction of seeing Goldsworthy straighten in his own chair so that they sat eye to eye.

"I take it Ravenhurst and Chartwell intended to bait a trap with some minor document."

"Did they get their man?"

"There was a complication when Lady Ravenhurst objected to having her guests searched as they left the party."

"Ah." Goldsworthy moved a pile of papers from one side of the vast desk to the other. "Did this fellow slip through the trap then?"

"The 'bait' is back in Lord Ravenhurst's library."

"What?" That got the big man's attention.

"In the coat closet I found two pages rolled up and stuffed in a finger of a man's glove, tucked in the outer pocket of a greatcoat."

"Our man's glove? How did he slip through?" Goldsworthy frowned.

"The fellow's name is Archer." Lynley watched to see whether Goldsworthy reacted to the name. Not a twitch. "His pocket, but not his glove. Archer's not our man."

"You'd best be certain of that, lad."

In Lynley's mind it wasn't as simple as Ravenhurst and Chartwell had supposed. "Archer is one of Lady Ravenhurst's flirts."

After Lynley had sent Emily Radstock home, he followed Archer and his friend to a gaming establishment, where they entered into several rounds of deep play. Archer never touched the gloves in his pocket. "If he has a role to play in the game, my guess is that he's a courier, and an unwitting one, at that. I doubt he has any idea that he may have been used to move documents."

"But he was not used to move them, as apparently you intervened." Goldsworthy's voice was a roar of displeasure probably heard all the way to Piccadilly. His large hands hit the table, making inkpots and pens bounce.

Lynley shrugged. He objected to clumsiness and cruelty. Ravenhurst's ruse would not have worked because Lynley was certain that the papers had been taken some time earlier and hidden in the cloakroom. No search of guests descending from the ballroom would have turned up the papers in the glove.

"Did I mention that there were two papers rolled inside the glove?"

"Two papers?"

Lynley reached into his waistcoat pocket and withdrew the scrap of paper he'd found curled up inside the document he'd returned to Ravenhurst's library. He tossed it onto the big man's desk. Goldsworthy snatched it up and spread it out under his big hands.

"I depend on you," Goldsworthy read. He looked up at Lynley. "What do you make of it?"

Lynley had been pondering that question with the part of his brain that remained functioning after Emily Radstock's kiss. He doubted that Archer was the "you" upon whom the writer of the note depended. Archer had left the party to spend an evening in careless play and deep drinking. Nor was there anyone at the gaming club with whom Archer had exchanged a word other than to place his bets or summon more spirits.

The "I" of the note was still more of a mystery, given the number of guests and servants present at Lady Ravenhurst's party. What Lynley could be sure of was that a degree of intimacy existed between the sender and the intended receiver of the note. No names were required between them. They had a plan, and they trusted one another.

"Depend on our mystery man to do what?" Goldsworthy asked.

"There must be an expected return. The documents must be in exchange for something."

"Money?" Goldsworthy quirked a shaggy brow. "The Russians pay well."

"Only if one of the guests is rather desperate, I'd say."

"We have to find those papers, lad, and we can't have our men..."

"Thinking on their own?"

"...bolloxing up the job when the traitor was ours for the taking."

Lynley hid a smile. He thought he'd handled Ravenhurst's wrong-headed scheme rather well. It was the kiss he'd bungled. He had meant to kiss Emily Radstock, lightly, playfully, to plant a distracting but forgettable peck on that quick mouth of hers. Kissing was supposed to be fun. He had not meant to get himself so worked up. He was no monk, but he was not his uncle, either.

"Our man is out there." Goldsworthy frowned. "He came to the party and took the bait. We need to lure him back to Ravenhurst's library."

"Do you have the guest list, sir?" Lynley asked.

"I do." The big man managed to extract a paper from the piles around him and hand it across the desk.

Lynley stood, accepting the list and glancing at the names. "It's through Lady Ravenhurst that guests have access to the house. We'll watch her in the park or at home to see which of her particular friends might have connections to the Russians."

"You think our man is going to go after papers at a hen party?"

"Gentlemen call as often as ladies, and the library opens from the entry, very accessible."

"You'll call then?"

"With my betrothed. Perfectly acceptable. And we'll go for a drive in the park." At least in the park there would be no danger of getting Emily Radstock alone in a dark corner and kissing her senseless.

"I will put Wilde on to watching the house. See who comes and goes, that sort of thing. Our man will try again."

Chapter Five

So prejudiced is society in favor of a woman's marrying that the sole measure of her worth is a paltry hoop of gold upon her finger. A single miss, however lovely, intelligent, and virtuous, whose hand remains unadorned by such a bauble within a Season or two of her first appearance in the fashionable world, is regarded as flawed no matter her merits, while the plainest girl with the least figure and only modest accomplishments may lord it over all her companions when once she wears a gentleman's ring. To do so, however, is to fall into the grave error of supposing that a ring on one's finger is a triumph or a victory. Such thinking must inevitably undermine the very happiness the husband hunter seeks in marriage.

—*The Husband Hunter's Guide to London*

Lynley watched Emily Radstock apply a hoof pick to her mare's near hind foot. Another woman would have left the task to a groom. He could find no fault in the practiced care with which she handled her horse. Her voice soothed the mare, and she plainly knew what she was about as she worked to dig out dirt and stones. Her dark blue habit was cut close to her figure with skirts full enough to allow her more than a fashionable walk in the park. A flush in her cheeks and loose curling strands of honey-brown hair around her face told him she'd had a good ride. He envied her that.

It was the part of his agreement with Goldsworthy which chafed him the most that he had been required to leave Sultan at Lyndale Abbey. His black stallion was too easily recognizable as the horse that had figured in the recent exploits of the highwayman of the Aylesbury Road, as the constables had dubbed him.

Emily had tied her horse, a chocolate-colored mare with a black mane, to a post in the open area of the mews between the rows of stalls. With the morning sun just peeking over the rooftops, grooms and stable boys went about their business, taking no notice of the lady in their midst. Lynley leaned against the wall to watch.

She went about her work, oblivious of her surroundings, until he ventured a greeting. She started, turning toward him but keeping a secure hold on the horse's hoof.

"What are you doing here?"

"I couldn't stay away."

She regarded him narrowly. "I should think you would still be abed."

"Not when I might see you." The words sounded hollow in his ears. It was the sort of flirtatious thing his uncle might say to a tavern girl.

"Fustian," she said. Gently, she released the horse's hoof and moved to the off side. "You've never come here at this hour of the day to pour the butter boat over my head, and you can't imagine that I have any government papers on my person."

"You relieve my mind. I would hate to think that you made off with Lord Ravenhurst's documents under my nose."

"Did someone make off with them?" she asked, coming around the horse to toss the hoof pick into a pail and pick up a dandy brush.

"I came to ask if I might take you for a drive in the park this afternoon."

"I have a...a prior engagement." She moved the brush across the mare's back with short flicks.

"I believe our betrothal ends your obligations to other gentlemen."

She shot him a quick glance. "I didn't say I was meeting a man."

"Can you put this person off to another day?"

She laughed. "Oh, he is always available for a visit. He's in Marshalsea Prison for debt."

He had to admit she shocked him a little with her cheerful willingness to visit a notorious prison, but only a little. He'd read her letter to the *Times*. "Who is this gentleman in such uncongenial accommodations?"

"The Reverend Arthur Broome. Do you know of him?"

It was a test. She'd think more highly of him if he knew who Broome was, but he wouldn't pretend. He shook his head.

"He founded the Royal Society for the Prevention of Cruelty to Animals." She moved from her work with the dandy brush to a currycomb.

"A worthy cause. Are you a member of this society?"

Her brow furrowed at the question, and she looked away. "Ladies are not yet admitted to membership status. We have a different role."

"You pour tea and provide funds?" Lynley suspected that a society with its founder in debt was little more than a scheme to prey on the tenderheartedness of rich ladies.

"We write letters and pamphlets."

"Sounds safe...and..."

The currycomb made a few passes. "And?"

"Dull."

Her chin came up at that. "Easy for you to say." She drew a deep, bosom-lifting breath. "Being born both female and of a certain rank, one is not permitted the full range of action in the world." She shrugged. "So we do what we can."

"Much better to come with me then." He pushed away from the wall and came around the horse to stand beside her. The mare cocked an ear his way.

"What? So I can drop glassware down a stairwell?"

"You have to admit that you enjoyed it." He grinned at her.

Her gaze dropped, but she didn't deny it. "Why did you need me to do it, I wonder. What purpose did it serve?"

He reached up to give the mare a scratch behind her ears. "What's her name?"

"Circe, and you didn't answer my question."

"Didn't I?" He let his hand slide along the sun-warmed flank of the horse. "Does she deserve a witch's name?"

"Sometimes." She laughed and patted the mare's rump. "She appears docile, but she will surprise you when she wants her own way."

"Is that what you're doing? Trying to have your own way?"

She faced him. They were closer than he'd realized. She tapped him on the chest with the currycomb. "What I would like is answers to some very reasonable questions about your actions last night." *Tap.* "What were you doing when you disappeared from my side?" *Tap.* "How did you know where to find Lord Ravenhurst's missing papers?" *Tap.* "Why did you return them?" *Tap.* "Why—"

He caught and trapped her hand against his chest. The fine thread that had stretched between them from the moment he'd unfolded himself from Rosalind Villiers's couch caught and held, a single shining filament of need.

She stared at his mouth. Behind him a groom's coarse shout and the rattle of carriage wheels broke the moment. He released her hand, and she dropped it to her side.

He made himself answer lightly. "Suit yourself, but an hour in the park could get you the answers to your questions."

* * * *

Emily had long understood that Hyde Park at the fashionable hour of five in the afternoon was not the park of her morning rides. As London society from the lowest to the highest ranks streamed through the gates in carriages, on horseback, and on foot, the park's horizons shrank. One did not look up through the tracery of lofty trees, or out across rolling vistas of the faintest green. One did not hear the cries of birds, but the clatter of wheels and shouts of greeting. It was necessary to keep a sharp eye out for erratic drivers and the careless tide of humanity.

She squirmed a little on the seat of Lynley's neat curricle. With her mother away, she'd had her first chance to visit Arthur Broome in jail, yet she'd succumbed to the temptation to go driving with Lynley in the park. Curiosity about her fiancé was a character weakness she did not care to examine.

She had to admit that Lynley was a neat driver with a light hand to which the horses responded readily. She could not help admiring a man who treated his animals well. And of course a tall, darkly handsome man must be observed. Heads turned and ladies fell into conversation as they passed. She could not repress a twinge of satisfaction at the expression on the faces of certain of her old friends when they saw Lynley and realized that he must be the fiancé of whom they'd heard. To those ladies she gave a friendly wave.

"Enjoying yourself?" he asked.

"Am I so readable? It is the tallying hour." She straightened her spine. "A time for chalking up points. Everyone is busily measuring his neighbor's consequence in new equipages or horses or..."

"Fiancés?"

"Exactly."

"Anything I can do to add to your tally?"

"If you must know, there is an art to the whole business of parading. One has to be seen without appearing to notice that one is being observed. It's all a great strain on one's neck."

With a slight movement of his hands he made the horses dance a little in their traces, setting the harness jingling. His whole attention appeared focused on driving, but heads again turned their way.

When the horses settled back to a sedate pace, she was sorely tempted to poke him in the ribs with her parasol. "You know exactly how to draw attention without seeming to do so."

"And you apparently know how to court invisibility." He gave her outfit a severe frown. She had dressed in a fawn-colored spencer jacket and plain chocolate velvet bonnet, lined with pale green silk. "Is tallying points only for ladies?"

"At least I'm not wearing black." Emily saw no reason to tell him that he would score no points for being seen with a woman who had been on the shelf for nearly five Seasons.

"You were going to tell me what you were really doing at the Ravenhurst party last night," she said.

"Was I?" An approaching barouche caught his attention. The stately vehicle carried a petite iron-haired lady in a deep-wine-colored coat and hat, black feathers curling over the brim, with her hands stuffed into a black fur muff the size of small spaniel.

Lynley tried to turn his team around, but traffic would not permit the maneuver. Instead the barouche, with its diminutive passenger riding in state, pulled up beside them.

In courtesy Lynley was obliged to halt his team, his gaze fixed on the small woman. "My aunt, Lady Silsden," he said to Emily.

"Lynley," said the woman. "Is that your new fiancée?"

"Aunt, may I present Lady Emily Radstock."

His aunt waved a peremptory black-gloved hand, beckoning Emily to join her in the barouche. Lynley's groom went to the horses' heads, and Lynley jumped down to assist Emily in moving from their carriage to his aunt's.

"We'll take a turn about the park, and I shall return her to you, Lynley," Lady Silsden declared. She waved him away from the carriage.

"Yes, ma'am." He stood stiff and frowning. Emily had never seen him ill at ease. As the barouche jerked into motion, she turned to face the woman who had discomposed him.

"Let me look at you, girl. You are Candover's daughter?"

"I am, Lady Silsden."

"And you've accepted my nephew?"

"I have, ma'am."

Emily found herself subjected to an insolent scrutiny. For the second time in a quarter of an hour her fawn-colored jacket and plain bonnet provoked a frown.

"You seem a sensible girl. What were you thinking?"

"Ma'am?"

"There's no worse bargain for a lady of rank, and you must bear the brunt of the blame. Of course, your mother must answer for her part of this folly, too. To be away from home when a daughter faces a rogue like Lynley." Lady Silsden shook her head.

"Ma'am, do you truly suppose your nephew to be such a poor bargain?"

"Don't let that charming smile of his deceive you, miss. Lynley is an exceptionally lazy and wayward specimen of his sex. If you do not exercise all your will to curb his appetites and inclinations, he will be forever chasing after some freakish adventure in the name of...fun." Lady Silsden shuddered.

Emily looked down at her gloved hands to keep from grinning. "What do you recommend, ma'am?"

"I don't doubt he's up to his usual tricks. Constables came to my door a fortnight ago with shocking inquiries about a highwayman holding up the common stage on the Aylesbury Road. The common stage!"

"And you think Lynley might have been involved?" That did sound like Lynley. Emily could imagine his aunt's horror at their adventure of the previous night.

"It is exactly the sort of freak he'd be up to, and with that black horse of his."

"A black horse, ma'am?"

"That Spanish horse of his, Sultan. Don't let him fool you with his driving in the park. He knows nothing of duty or dignity. A baronet must be seen to live like a baronet. Not like a gypsy."

"How fortuitous to meet you, Lady Silsden. I can see that I must learn from you if I am to help Lynley maintain his credit as a gentleman in London. What do you recommend?"

Lady Silsden sighed. "I spent years after the disaster trying to curb his dangerous proclivities, and I might have succeeded had not my wretched brother-in-law intervened and taken the boy to Spain." She shuddered again.

Emily tucked the intriguing word *disaster* away in her mind. Instinctively, she knew Lynley would resent her hearing about it from his aunt. "And you feel thwarted in your efforts, ma'am?"

"I do. Horribly."

"What do you recommend I do to curb Lynley's dangerous tendencies toward..."

"Wickedness. There is no other word for it."

"Shall I take him to the Chapel Royal? Or do you recommend more extreme measures?"

"I don't mind telling you, Miss Radstock, for you seem to appreciate the situation, but in my view, no measure is too extreme. I confined the boy to his room at Lyndale. I restricted all foods that might inflame the passions. I hired tutors to read him the most powerful tracts on moral behavior. I surrounded him with the inspiration of the most saintly figures art has produced."

"I see," said Emily. Again she had recourse to staring at her hands lest she give away her feelings on Lady Silsden's program of moral improvement. "You have spared no effort to reform his character."

"Not as long as he was in my care."

"And how long was that, ma'am?"

"From the time he was fourteen until his eighteenth year. Sadly, in spite of all my efforts, he remains...volatile and given to behavior quite beneath the dignity of a baronet."

"Lady Silsden, thank you for confiding in me. I will give your counsel some thought and only hope that I may have some good effect on your nephew's character." That, at least, Emily could promise. She certainly had no intention of harming Lynley's character.

They had nearly completed their circuit of the park at a pace designed to put even Lady Silsden's placid horses to sleep. Emily could see Lynley, standing with a group of gentlemen around a woman holding court in another carriage. As they drew closer, she recognized Lady Ravenhurst, her golden beauty set off by a pale lilac pelisse and white muff.

Lady Silsden's barouche came to stop.

"I suppose, Miss Radstock, that you feel bound in conscience to continue this engagement you've formed."

"I do, ma'am."

"Well, do not worry. Look at him." She stared pointedly at the group of laughing gentlemen around Lady Ravenhurst. Lynley appeared as rapt in admiration as the others.

Lady Silsden harrumphed. She nodded to her footman, who lowered the steps and opened the door for Emily. Then Lady Silsden offered her last words of comfort. "I daresay this whim of Lynley's will pass soon enough, and you'll find yourself released."

Chapter Six

The husband hunter must be particularly on her guard when a new acquaintance, whether a lady or a gentleman, appears most open. The new friend who freely unfolds his or her history of misfortune and grievance, while entitled to polite sympathy, must be regarded with wariness. It is an easy step from engaging the husband hunter's sympathy to asking her to open not only her heart, but also her purse and her person.

—*The Husband Hunter's Guide to London*

From across the carriageway, Lynley spotted his aunt's footman handing Emily Radstock down from the barouche. He stepped away from Lady Ravenhurst's carriage. Emily said nothing as he took her hand, her alert gaze on Lady Ravenhurst's admirers. In silence Lynley handed her up to the curricle seat, leaped up to take the reins, and set the carriage in motion.

He guided the horses, avoiding other vehicles and riders out of habit, surprised at her silence. In the two days they'd been acquainted, he thought he could count on her to tell him what she was thinking. Beside him she closed and unclosed her gloved hands.

"Was my aunt Silsden sufficiently frank to put you off our engagement?" he asked.

She tugged at one of her gloves, freeing the hand that wore his ring and stretching out her arm to look at the stones, the diamonds flashing around the great square amethyst.

He kept his hands easy on the reins, waiting for her to pull the thing off and slap it in his hand. It would not matter to his happiness, of course.

He would pocket the ring, return her to her family, and find a different cover for his movement in society. Their brief engagement would be a bit of tittle-tattle for a few days before another scandal displaced theirs.

Abruptly, she turned to him, her eyes flashing. "Your aunt would make a fine elephant keeper. She appears well versed in the techniques of confinement and deprivation, and she would not hesitate to shoot you if you got out of line."

"So I'm an elephant?" he said.

"Hardly, but you must have towered over your aunt even at fourteen. She probably mistook that height of yours for power."

His jaw tightened. "What did my aunt say to you?"

She grinned at him, a defiant look in her eyes. "You'd like to know, wouldn't you?"

Then she dropped her bare hand with the ring and let it dangle over the side of the carriage for all to see.

Even Lynley knew she was behaving outrageously. Older ladies in passing carriages stiffened in outrage, while younger ladies gawked. One young woman in a close-fitting gold jacket that emphasized the striking dimensions of her chest gave Emily a particularly hard look.

"So you're keeping the ring?" he asked.

She nodded. "Lynley, do you own a hair shirt by any chance?"

"My tailor does not supply them."

"It's only that I thought you might be needing one to repent the fun you had last night."

"Fun?"

"Your aunt has a particularly dim view of fun. And I feel certain that she would strongly condemn your sneaking about at a dinner party, recovering missing government papers and feigning imbecility, that sort of thing."

"You call that fun?" His fiancée was too perceptive. He would have to distract her from his spy activities.

His baser self immediately suggested a way he could do that. He had not at first imagined taking liberties with her beyond an occasional kiss on her hand. There would be no harm in such practiced gallantry. But in the dark, in the gap between the ballroom doors after she had moved with him so perfectly through the dance, he had been moved to kiss her properly.

"You were quite busy all evening," she said, "and I gather there was more to do after you bundled me into my carriage. Did you return to Lady Ravenhurst?"

"Lady Ravenhurst?" Maybe his fiancée did not suspect him of spying after all, but of having a flirt.

"I wonder what brought her to the park. She has no need of a husband."
Lynley asked, "You think she should stay home?"

A headshake was her reply. "Not at all. But as my *Husband Hunter's Guide* points out, being seen in an open barouche in the park is essential to husband-hunting. So I wonder what brings Lady Ravenhurst to gather gentlemen around her when she already possesses a husband."

"Some women never outgrow their passion for admiration." Lynley's uncle firmly believed that passion to be the great weakness of beautiful women, one to be exploited at every opportunity.

Emily shrugged. "She's lovely, of course, but she's too unhappy to care for compliments."

"I thought she was taking great pleasure in the gallantries tossed her way."

Emily shook her head, her expression now grave. "I suspect that her pleasure is entirely artificial. Whatever is making her unhappy, I'll wager you that she'd prefer to go home, throw herself on her bed, weep her heart out, and consume a platter of cream puffs, rather than smile and accept tributes from a group of gentlemen who prefer their women decorative, demure, and domestic."

Once she said it, Lynley saw that it was true. Lady Ravenhurst's public gaiety was false.

He had guessed as much the night before. So why had she come to the park? The most likely answer was that she came to meet someone. The puzzle intrigued him. He wondered if Lady Ravenhurst were in the power of some spy. A brief meeting in the park, as if by chance, without apparent concealment, would be an opportunity to pass information. Gloves, papers, messages, all could be exchanged while what appeared to happen was mere flirtation.

As far as Lynley knew, none of the gentlemen currently around her had any known ties to England's enemies. A poke in the ribs brought him back to the present.

"Do you have any other relations who might accost me in the park?" she asked.

"None."

"Your aunt does not have children of her own?"

"None."

"And your uncle?"

"Never married."

"Lynley, you must do your share to keep the conversation going. Tell me something about last night, or take me home," she said.

What could he tell her? Goldsworthy would insist he tell her nothing. The public was not to know that spies or their counterparts existed in London. She sighed. "You did not stumble upon the missing papers. You were nosing about before we overheard the Ravenhursts arguing."

"Ah, but I overheard Ravenhurst earlier in the evening. I could tell the plan was flawed, and if I could see that, so could the intended target. It was doomed and would only cause...the lady trouble."

"So you took it upon yourself to intervene?"

"The plan seemed likely to cause unnecessary distress without solving the government's problem."

"What is the problem? Do you know?"

He shrugged, but did not meet her gaze. "Where may I escort you tonight?"

"To the opera. In my mother's absence I must host her usual party, but I warn you, Lynley, do not try another disappearing act."

"So, no chance to drop glassware down a stairwell or hide in a closet. However will we manage to amuse ourselves?"

A little shiver was the only sign she gave of her reaction to the idea. She brought her hand back to her lap and put on her glove, and he guided them out of the park.

* * * *

The afternoon post brought a letter from Emily's mother.

My dear Emily,

I hear from your father and your sister that you may have taken my gift of a guidebook too much to heart, and in your characteristic way have thrown yourself into an engagement with a man quite unknown to your family. Please do not order any wedding clothes without consulting me first.

You may rest assured that I will return to London as soon as your grandmother's health improves.

As ever,
Your loving mother

* * * *

Lynley found the opera instructive—not the story of the fairy king Oberon's efforts to regain the affections of his queen through the manipulation of mere mortals, but the display of London society. Bright chandeliers exposed the crowd as well as the performers. From the vast floor up to the tiers of boxes with their red hangings and gilt edges, the Royal Opera House, like the park, was a place for the fashionable to see and be seen.

The scene was nothing like the *café cantantes* of Jerez, dark and intimate, where he had often escaped from his uncle to listen to a lone guitarist or watch a single dancer.

Lynley's gaze passed over the crowd. After years in Spain, he could name perhaps only a score of people in the boxes. He needed to do better to find the missing government papers. One fellow particularly intrigued him, a silver-haired gentleman nearer to fifty than forty, dressed with attention to the latest mode, who sat at Lady Ravenhurst's left elbow in a box across the theater.

It was apparent from the moment the gentleman entered the box that he had some hold over the lady. Lynley's thoughts on the matter were interrupted by the interval and the arrival in their box of a young man from his distant school days, Roddy Twedell.

"Thought it was you, Lynley. Heard you'd returned from somewhere or other."

"Spain."

"You've let yourself be caught already, I hear," Twedell remarked, glancing at Emily Radstock. "Saw the notice in the papers that you'll be buckled soon."

"You may congratulate me."

"Never thought that one would marry. Heard she wouldn't be under anyone's thumb. Well, to each his own, but if you want to sample something rather different, let me know. And come by the club. You can tell me about those sherries of Spain."

"It's a Palo Cortado you want, Twedell."

* * * *

Emily's duties as hostess to those of her mother's friends who made up the party kept her busy at the interval, making sure chairs were rearranged and everyone had a lemonade or a wine and some cake from a tray of refreshments. When she looked up from a conversation with one of her mother's oldest friends, she was surprised to see her brother-in-law, who was no opera lover.

"Em," said Phil, eying the tiny cakes and tarts on the refreshment tray. "Came for Roz, she wants to know if you did something...indelicate in the park today."

"Do have a tart, Phil," Emily suggested. "What makes Roz think that?"

"Miss Throckmorton called. Do you know her?"

"I think everyone does."

"Thing is, Roz doesn't want your mama to hear anything to...worry her, you know."

"There is nothing to worry about, Phil. Miss Throckmorton probably saw me waving Lynley's ring about in my excitement over our engagement." At the moment, Lynley's gaze was fixed intently on Lady Ravenhurst's box. Emily turned her back on her fiancé. Better not to watch.

"Phil, do you know Lynley's aunt Silsden?"

Phil shuddered. "Terrible woman. Best to avoid her. Didn't like Lynley going to school. She had to let him go, of course. His father's will and all."

"Well, I met her today in the park. What did she mean by the *disaster*? What happened to Lynley?"

Phil shook his head, his hand hovering over a tart. "Can't tell you, Em. Don't worry about Lynley, great tall fellow like him will always take care of himself."

"When did he get his height, Phil?"

Phil appeared to consider the question, though his gaze was still on the tart. "Always taller than me."

"And Spain? Why did he go to Spain?"

"You know, Em, you should ask Lynley these questions."

"I will. I just don't want to be wholly ignorant."

"Lynley's uncle took him to Spain, straight out of Cambridge. We'd just begun, but the uncle said college was no education for a man of the world."

"So what kind of education did the uncle want for him?"

Phil shook his head. "Don't know. Lynley never talks about Spain, except about sherry and horses. Marvelous horses, the Andalusians. Did you know monks bred and trained them before Napoleon tried to steal them, and these brothers, the Zamoras, hid a herd?"

"Monks?"

"Yes." Phil chose the tart he wanted from the plate. "Lynley has a stallion from Spain. Can't bring him to town though. Keeps him at Lyndale Abbey."

The tart disappeared, and Phil's gaze returned to the plate. "Thing is, Roz has been eating so little, we haven't had..."

"Cake, Phil?" Emily wanted to keep her brother-in-law talking about his friend. The big mystery remained the "disaster" that had put a fourteen-year-old boy in the care of a censorious aunt and then a profligate uncle. Obviously, part of the disaster was the death of Lynley's father. No mention had been made of his mother.

In the park Emily had not wanted him to know how shocking she'd found his aunt's revelations. She had made light of what he'd endured for the four years he'd been in Lady Silsden's care, but the harsh regimen of scolds and restrictions could not have been easy for a young man of spirit to endure.

Emily tried to reconcile the two different pictures she had of him. On the one hand was the man who appeared utterly imperturbable, the sort who would face cannon fire with a quip and a perfectly arranged neckcloth; on the other hand was the boy who must have suffered at the hands of relations who had used him as a rope in a tug-of-war for family power.

"When did Lynley return from Spain?"

"Must have been several months back. Didn't see him until he came to town a fortnight ago." Phil brushed cake crumbs from his mouth. "You two are hitting it off, are you?"

"Perfectly," said Emily. She glanced at her fiancé. Once again he stood watching the golden beauty in the opposite box.

* * * *

Lynley caught Phil just as his friend stepped out of the Candover box. "Not staying for act two?" he asked.

Phil shook his head.

"Coward."

"Don't care for opera. Just came to check on Em for Roz. Don't want Roz to worry. In her condition and all."

"Very proper, Phil. And should Roz worry?"

Phil's smooth brow wrinkled. "Em says you two are getting along perfectly and that she did nothing...indelicate in the park today."

It was another lesson about London. Inevitably, one's smallest indiscretion was observed. What happened in the park in the afternoon became the evening's gossip.

"Phil, I won't keep you, but I need a quick favor. There is a gentleman whose name I need to know."

They reentered the box, standing in the shadows at the back as the second act began on the stage below. Lynley pointed out the gentleman sitting at Lady Ravenhurst's elbow just as the man placed a hand on her shoulder and leaned forward to whisper something in her ear.

Phil stiffened beside him. "That's Barksted."

"Who is he?"

"A gamester. A very rum touch. I should think Ravenhurst would toss the fellow out of the box."

"Ravenhurst isn't there," Lynley pointed out.

Phil peered at the box again. "So he's not. Well, I wouldn't want a fellow like that around Roz, I can tell you."

"Why not?"

Phil shook his head. "He's not a cheat or a sharp exactly, at least no one's caught him at it, but he likes to hold on to a person's vowels and make them sweat. He's a squeezer, that's what he is."

Lynley thought Phil was right, but if the pressure on Lady Ravenhurst came from a mere card sharp, not a foreign spy, Lynley had gone down a blind alley in his search for the missing papers.

"Where does Barksted like to play, Phil?"

"Private house in St. James's, I imagine."

"The one run by that female, Mrs. Hewitt?"

"Yes, do you know it?"

"I was there last night." Lynley had not seen Barksted there, but he'd like to find out how the man operated.

"Must get back to Roz, Lynley."

"Go." Lynley clapped Phil on the shoulder. "But meet me at Mrs. Hewitt's establishment after the opera. Shall we say one?"

Phil groaned. "Lynley, I'm an old married man. I'm going to be a father."

"There's bound to be an excellent supper at two."

Lynley remained at the back of the box while the soprano on the stage poured out an aria. The vast audience suspended most conversation to listen. When the crowd applauded, he moved to return to his seat and found himself caught in Emily Radstock's gaze. The look in her eyes and the proud tilt of her head told him that while apparently occupied with her duties as a hostess, she had missed none of his actions in the interval. It was time to distract her.

Chapter Seven

We are used in our present age to think of a betrothal as a bargain. In families of means the lawyers meet to negotiate the settlements almost before the sweet kiss of a lady's acceptance fades from the lips of her betrothed. The contract between parties who are to share life's deepest joys and sorrows appears to be a matter of dowries, jointures, and provisions for offspring. When the ink is dry on these documents, it is impossible to break with one another without facing a protracted legal contest. No doubt many enter into marriage as into a bargain, but how much more like a true marriage might it be to consider the betrothal like a solemn covenant.

—*The Husband Hunter's Guide to London*

By the time the knight Haroun and the princess Reiza had been tied to a stake to be burned and the fairy queen and king had been summoned to intervene, Emily had quite lost the thread of their adventures. It was Lynley's fault. She had warned him not to disappear. Instead he'd dominated her senses with his nearness.

He adjusted her wrap, his gloved fingers trailing down her shoulder. He whispered a question about Puck's singing, his breath disturbing the curls over her ears. His knee collided with hers as he adjusted his chair to make room for his long legs. His hand brushed hers as he consulted the program. Whenever she turned to remonstrate with him, her gaze went to his wonderful crooked mouth, just inches from her face.

She knew what he was up to. He wanted her to forget the attention he had paid to the blond beauty across the theater. Instead her body shook like a teapot on the boil with awareness of him. She tried to fix her attention on her mother's friends, saying her goodnights and thanking them for coming, but with Lynley at her side, she bungled the simplest goodbyes. And then they were in the carriage, the dark, close carriage, rocking along. She scooted to the far side of the bench.

"Em," he said, "I did not disappear tonight."

"Thank you for that." She was conscious of a slight quiver in her voice. Their engagement gave him the privilege of her name, and at once he had shortened it to one drawn-out syllable.

He reached out and pulled her toward him. She resisted briefly, then let herself be drawn. He tilted her chin up with one gloved hand and lowered his mouth to hers. It was just the touch her senses had clamored for through the evening.

She did not recognize her firm, practical mouth. Her perfectly serviceable lips, which she counted on to admit modest amounts of air and sustenance, now became greedy, as if nothing but the taste of Lynley could satisfy their hunger. The sensation rushed not along the paths of her nerves, but shot straight to her heart, jolting it out of a long sleep.

Emily wrenched her mouth from his and pushed against his chest. His arms released her, and she tumbled back on the seat. She straightened.

"You're thinking," he said, his voice a low rasp.

"Of course I'm thinking. You only kiss me to interfere with the working of my brain. What is your fascination with Lady Ravenhurst? Is she the lost love of your youth? Or do you suspect her of concealing government documents in that little blue velvet reticule of hers with the silver ties?"

"Neither. I thought you enjoyed our kisses last night."

"I don't deny it. You obviously know what you're about. But you put a ring on my finger, kiss me senseless, show me the pain that could be ours in marriage, and shove me in a carriage alone? What were you thinking?"

"Considering the alternative, it seemed the wisest course?"

"What alternative? Attentive, gallant behavior?"

"Ravishing you in a carriage."

"People do not engage in...carnal congress in carriages with coachmen on the box and footmen riding behind, besides linkboys and who knows who else about and the discomforts and..."

"Oh, but they do. Consult your guidebook. I think you'll find that the author advises against being alone in a closed carriage with a man."

Emily certainly knew the essential mechanics of carnal embrace. She'd read the radical pamphlets written for poor women on the subject of cundoms. And the outraged letters to the *Times* about those pamphlets. She just hadn't imagined until this moment in Lynley's presence the gap between reading about the subject and engaging in the activity. And there was another gap she had not considered—the gap between sitting upright and fully clothed in conversation with a man and lying unclothed with him for a different form of intercourse.

"You're thinking again."

"I'm trying to understand how it can be managed."

"Trust me. It can be done."

"But you don't mean to do it." She shook her head to rid it of confusion. "You kiss to distract me. You could simply say that you don't wish me to pry."

"I don't wish you to pry into my interest in Lady Ravenhurst. There, I've said it. Now, can we go back to where we were?" He reached for her again.

Emily held him off with a hand pressed against his chest. "We can't continue an engagement, even such an engagement as ours, if you have a romantic interest in another woman, a married woman, at that."

"I don't," he said.

She let her hand drop. His denial sounded sincere. She wished she could see his face properly. The fleeting play of light and shadow in the dark carriage made a searching inquiry of a man's face impossible. Gentlemen were supposed to be free, after certain marital obligations had been met, to pursue other interests. It should not bother her, but Emily did not wish to contemplate Lynley pursuing Lady Ravenhurst. But if he was telling her the truth, she must draw a different conclusion. "Then you are a...spy?"

"Spy?"

"What would you call it? You are someone who does the government's work. You've hatched some kind of plan with Phil."

"You can't imagine that Phil has anything to do with spying."

"No, of course not." When he put it like that, the whole idea seemed absurd. But she knew how to test him. "Ride with me in the morning."

There was a pause before he said, "Yes."

"Circe and I will be ready at seven." If he had some plan with Phil that would keep them out until the small hours of the morning, he would hardly agree to meet her so early.

"Seven it is," he said.

Chapter Eight

There is in human society a tendency for the fortunate among us to mistake our favorable circumstances for superiority of character. And to consider those whom circumstance places beneath us as deserving of their position though fortune is wholly external to either party. While it is unlikely that the husband hunter will encounter genuine vice in her Season, London, like any great city, has its unsavory neighborhoods where the merely unfortunate and the actively ill-intentioned mingle.

—*The Husband Hunter's Guide to London*

The widowed Mrs. Hewitt, who, as Phil explained, had once been quite respectable, now ran an elegant little gaming establishment on a quiet street off St. James's Square. Lynley had seen most of its rooms the night before. The club had a faro bank, a spinning EO wheel, and rooms for several varieties of card play. The supper was passable, but he could have advised their hostess on her choice of wines. There was not an acceptable sherry in her cellar.

Greeting them, their amiable hostess explained certain house policies, including a rule against smoking. She said she would not have her drapery reeking of smoke. Lynley gave Phil a small stake for the faro table, told him not to lose too much, and made a complete circuit of the other rooms. There was no sign of Archer and his friend from the evening before, no sign of documents being exchanged, no one speaking Russian, merely Englishmen careless of their fortunes, willing to risk vast sums on the turn of a card. Again, Lynley had to concede that so far the leads he'd followed from Lady Ravenhurst's party had led nowhere. He did find the lady herself at Barksted's side in a room devoted to hazard.

The only woman at a table with six gentlemen, Lady Ravenhurst eagerly took the dice cup in hand and declared a main of eight. She rolled a nick to win her stake and barely paused to scrape her winnings toward Barksted before declaring another main. She rolled the chance three times, winning a streak of side bets, before losing her turn to the fellow on her left. Her spirits seemed to ride on the rattle of the dice in the leather cup, their tumble across the green baize, and the pair of numbers facing up. She reminded Lynley of a rider galloping neck or nothing at a fence, and he knew she wanted only to roll again.

After play had gone round the table, the group paused to refill glasses. Lynley did not know how badly she was dipped, but she turned to Barksted, appealing to him to stake her to another round. The man smiled and produced a roll of the ready from an inner pocket. She laughed, snatched at the roll, and withdrew to the ladies' retiring room.

Lynley knew boredom. He knew restrictions. He knew the exhilaration of breaking out of one's bonds. And he knew that losing and borrowing to play again was a sure trap. Nothing put a person in another's power like borrowing blunt you could not return.

Minutes later, Lady Ravenhurst emerged from attending to her toilette, and frowned when she saw Lynley. "What are you doing here?"

"I came to escort you home whenever you're ready to leave."

Her mouth closed in a stubborn line. "I'll not be going home until after supper."

"Supper is available now if you'd let me escort you."

"Pardon me." Mrs. Hewitt's voice came from behind him.

Lynley turned to find his hostess unsmiling, no longer cordial.

"I must ask you to leave, Sir Lynley. The club does not provide refreshment for those who do not play," she said.

Barksted stood behind Mrs. Hewitt, and behind him stood Phil, holding their hats and coats and looking most uneasy.

"I'm ready if you are, Lynley," Phil called.

Instinct rebelled against leaving any woman, no matter how lost in folly, with Barksted. Lynley hardly knew the man, but he did not doubt his power over Lady Ravenhurst. Still he knew better than to try to separate a woman from the passion that drove her. That was a lesson he'd learned early in life.

Lynley bowed to the ladies.

Outside the club Phil fixed his hat on his head. "Glad to be out of there. Breathe fresh air."

London was hardly noted for its fresh air, but Lynley knew what Phil meant. The night felt cool and clean after Mrs. Hewitt's stale rooms.

"Ugly customer, that Barksted," said Phil. "Has Mrs. Hewitt in his pocket, I suspect."

"Mrs. Hewitt?" Lynley woke the hackney driver waiting for them.

Phil nodded. "Saw Barksted set Mrs. Hewitt on you."

"Thanks, Phil. That's most helpful."

Phil shrugged. "Friends, don't you know." He climbed into the hackney and looked back at Lynley. "You're walking?" He sounded uneasy. "I don't like it."

"Only a few blocks. It'll clear my head." He waved Phil off. The carriage pulled away, the rumble of its wheels receding as it turned the corner.

Lynley started walking. He needed to think about the case. He had been certain when he'd joined the spy club that he would have no trouble finding the missing documents. His brief stint as a highwayman had ended, and he had blithely signed the year-and-a-day agreement that governed Goldsworthy's spies, thinking only of the lark it would be. That was before he'd met Emily Radstock. She had an unexpected ability to distract him, and yet she seemed dangerously alert to his actions.

He had nearly reached Piccadilly when late bells rang the hour with remarkable unison from a half dozen or more nearby churches. As he turned into the short, dark block of Bennet Street, the peals faded, and he heard heavy footsteps close in on him from behind.

He spun around, flinging up his left hand and taking a blow to the forearm from a short club. His hat went flying. He aimed his right fist at his assailant's jaw. Fist and bone collided with a jarring impact that sent the man staggering backward into a second fellow. The second man flung the first aside and came after Lynley like a bull, head down. Lynley stepped aside, letting the man plow with a heavy thud into the brick façade of a shop.

The second man grunted and rolled to one side, leaning against the bricks, his breath coming in thick pants.

Lynley lunged forward. His evening shoes slipped on the cobbles, and he went down hard. He scrambled up, quick, but not quick enough. His assailants had cut him off, one on either side of him, blocking the ends of the street. They were indistinguishable, compact and brutish, dressed in layers of rough, dark clothing, hats pulled low over their brows, hands in leather gloves. They knew their business.

Lynley could handle one of them easily enough, but two would be difficult. In his evening clothes and shoes, he was at a further disadvantage. In the light of a single street lamp he saw no weapon other than the short club in the first man's hand, but he wouldn't put it past the second fellow to produce a blade.

His pulse raced. His heart pounded. He made himself think in spite of his body's clamor for action. Neither of them had spoken. There had been no demand for his blunt. They had not, then, been lying in wait to relieve some gentleman of his purse on the way home from a night's gaming.

"Tell Barksted," Lynley said, "that his methods won't stop me."

"Yer a cheeky one ta give orders," the second man said, but he did not deny the Barksted connection. He nodded to his companion, and the two began to close in on Lynley.

Lynley removed one of his useless shoes and tossed it at the single lamp illuminating the scene. Glass shattered, and the flame flickered and went out. He pressed back in the shadow of the building.

The shuffling of his attackers' feet sounded loud in his ears. He had only delayed the inevitable. He guessed they meant to give him a beating as a warning not to interfere at the club with whatever it was that Barksted had going.

"Where is 'e?" one of the men said.

"Between us, ye nodcock. Keep movin' in."

The attack when it came was a flurry of kicks and blows, grunts and thuds. Lynley kept his back to the wall, his arms up in a fighting stance. His ribs and forearms took most of the punishment. He kept thinking about how long they would keep it up and how much punishment he could deal out in return.

He realized they wanted him to go down, but refused to give them the satisfaction. He wanted blood. With an upward backhanded swing of his left fist he caught one man's nose. The man's head snapped back. The crack of his nose mingled with his yelp of pain, and a spray of blood hit Lynley as the man reeled away. The other man cursed and drove in on Lynley, furiously swinging his club.

Lynley started to go down under the blows when a flash of light caught the attacker's face as a hackney came round the corner. The driver drove right at them, and the attacker scurried back, lifting his companion by his collar and hauling the man up. They stumbled off in the dark as the hackney stopped in front of Lynley.

A man jumped down from the passenger seat.

"Phil, is that you?" Lynley asked.

"Came back. Didn't like you walking."

"Thanks."

"Let's get you home."

"Gladly." Suddenly, Lynley was aware of all the places that hurt. He would not be riding with Emily Radstock at seven.

Chapter Nine

The plainest girl from the grandest manor or the most
insignificant cottage longs from an early age to be a bride. The
sun of her imagined wedding day casts bright beams over the
lesser, unmarked days of her girlhood. In the manor she tries
on the veil and coronet preserved by mother and grandmother.
Beyond the cottage gate she gathers wildflowers to carry down
weedy aisles. Wandering on her own, she writes new names for
herself with a stick in church registries on the banks of streams.
She is a mere girl. No one sees the vivid life within her. No one
notes her capacity for love. Yet she never doubts that she is
meant to be seen, known, loved, and chosen. She is meant to be
a bride.

—*The Husband Hunter's Guide to London*

Emily poked at the eggs on her plate, round and perfect, crisp on the edges, white with dark yellow centers, a well-matched pair.

Generally, she liked breakfast. A lady could almost always eat breakfast in the privacy of her family's morning room without anyone commenting on what or how much she consumed, while at a dinner or a ball, the lady of delicacy and sensibility must appear to exist on air. Nothing substantial could touch her lips. She could not be caught in the act of chewing. Emily had not chewed a morsel in public in her first three Seasons.

This morning, disappointment lodged in her throat. In the carriage after the opera she had guessed that Lynley was preparing for some adventure. He had the kind of energy that required action. And the whole point of trying to kiss her had clearly been to distract her so that she would not, could not, think about his real object in becoming engaged to her.

She broke the yellow center of one of her eggs and dipped a corner of toast in it. This morning she had to face facts. She had let herself be seduced by the idea of being engaged. It mortified her to realize that dangling her ring over the side of Lynley's carriage, catching the envious looks of girls still waiting for their moment, she had been as caught up in bride fever as the greenest girl in her first Season.

In Emily's case the ring on her finger was a hollow show. It had changed nothing. She had her life. Lynley had his. She had letters to write and people to meet. Arthur Broome was still in Marshalsea Prison. Lynley probably had a pressing need to stroll down to his club. A two-day engagement did not mean either of them had to change plans made previously. She should simply ignore him and go about her day as if his failing to ride with her made no difference to her life.

She jabbed the remaining yolk. She could just imagine him lying in bed, his dark hair tousled, his long limbs tangled in sheets and coverlet, his eyes closed with the dark lashes down across his cheeks, and his beautiful crooked mouth slightly open. Best not to think about Lynley's mouth. The thought made her conscious of her own mouth.

She blinked. April sunshine streamed through the morning room windows. Her father sat at his end of the table behind the *Chronicle*, drinking his tea. It was like dining alone. She could break crockery or set the room on fire before Papa would look up. Pressing matters of national finance and threats of war occupied his mind, not a superfluous unmarried daughter.

There had been a time when Papa, Mama, and their three offspring— Emily, Frederick, and Roz—had all taken breakfast together, and Mama had banished the paper and insisted on conversation. They had been children then. Now Roz and Frederick had homes of their own. It was only Emily who remained in her childhood place. No wonder her father took no notice of her. She was supposed to be elsewhere. And now that she was engaged, her father truly had no need to concern himself with her.

"The opera party went well, Papa," Emily said.

Behind the *Chronicle* her father gave no sign of hearing her. She pushed away from the table.

"I think I'll find Lynley this morning and break a vase over his head." She had no idea where Lynley lodged. She could neither send a message nor go round to pound on his door until his servants admitted her.

The paper rustled in her father's hands. He mumbled something.

Emily stood and took a last reluctant look at her eggs. "Of course, I don't know where Lynley lodges, so I may be obliged to wander about London with the appropriate vase for some time. I was thinking of the two-handled, Sphinx-headed blue pot in the second drawing room. It's time for Mama to redecorate, don't you think?"

The newspaper came down a bit. She could see her father's brown hair, wrinkled brow, and puzzled blue eyes. "Your mother has decorating plans?"

Emily smiled. It occurred to her where she could go to find Lynley. Phil would know. "As soon as she comes home."

Her father lowered his paper to the table. "Are you off then, Em?"

"I'm going to look in on Roz."

Her father nodded, and the paper came back up.

* * * *

A footman admitted Emily to the house, explaining that Mr. Gittings was not available. Tugging at her bonnet strings, Emily assured him that she knew her way to the morning room.

"No one's about, miss," the footman said. "Breakfast has been put back on account of the master's guest."

"Guest?" Emily removed her gloves and cloak.

"In the drawing room, miss."

"Thank you. I'll see myself up." Emily smiled and handed her gloves and cloak to the footman as if she were paying an ordinary morning call. She could think of only one guest who would make himself free with Roz's drawing room.

The room lay hushed, cool, and dark and apparently deserted, no fire yet lit in the hearth. A single shaft of light where the drapery panels did not meet made a bright path across the pale blue carpet. Emily closed the door behind her and stood listening. From behind the curved back of the large green sofa came the faint rumble of a mild snore.

She crossed the room and peeked over the sofa back. There was her fiancé, lying just where he'd been hiding the day they met. Her stomach dropped the way it did when she and Circe took a jump. She clenched her fists to keep from reaching down to touch him.

The oversized sofa was made to hold him. He lay on his back in his black evening trousers and white shirt, his cloak over him, one arm across the cloak. He was shoeless, and the black silk stockings on his long, elegant feet were shredded and streaked with dirt and blood. Spatters of blood dotted the linen of his shirt at the open collar.

A night's growth of beard shadowed his jaw, and a purple bruise the size of a thrush egg swelled there. He had plainly been in a fight, though where and how he'd lost his shoes in the fray, Emily could not imagine. He was deeply asleep. When he woke, she suspected he'd be in need of a saline draft for the aches.

She pulled up a chair. She meant to get answers to her questions about his sudden appearance in London, his hasty engagement to her, his interest in Lady Ravenhurst, and his habit of provoking chaos. But first she could really look at him without the cool front he showed to her or the imbecilic pose he wore in society.

He moaned, stretched, and opened one eye briefly.

"Good morning. I imagine your aches and pains are making themselves known."

His eyes opened. "You." The word was a dry croak. He swallowed. "How..."

"Roz and Phil are my family, you know." Emily stood and crossed the room to ring the bell. "Tell me what you need."

He groaned.

"Something cold and wet?" she asked.

She heard a vaguely affirmative mumble and sent the wide-eyed footman who answered the bell for a few items she thought would be helpful.

She settled beside him again. He opened his eyes. "I missed our ride."

"And sent no message."

"My apologies."

"I'm curious to know how you lost your shoes." She did not ask him if he'd won the fight.

His crooked mouth quirked slightly in what might have been a smile. "You're curious about more than that."

"Well yes, I am. As your fiancée, a position which, by the way, seems to require a lot of looking the other way while you do whatever it is you really came to London to do, I'd like to know what, besides a spectacular bosom and an idiot husband, draws you to Lady Ravenhurst."

He laughed lightly, which made him wince and press his hand to his ribs. He swung his feet to the floor and pushed himself up. The cloak slipped from his shoulders. His shirt hung loose and open at the throat and cuffs. He smelled of warm linen and himself. He took a moment to steady himself, his hands gripping the edge of the sofa. He seemed to have all his teeth, and his nose looked as straight and perfect as it had the day before.

All Emily's questions rushed in on her. How had he come by his imperfect mouth and his indifference to opinion? What disaster had left him under his aunt's dominion while still a boy?

The footman returned with the tray Emily had requested, and she occupied herself setting it down on a table near the green sofa. "Tankard or saline draft?" she asked.

"Tankard."

"Was Phil part of this melee?" she asked.

Lynley took a swallow of the ale. She watched his throat work, surprised at her interest in a part of him usually swathed in linen. "I owe him. He broke it up."

"And where were you? There are parts of London where unaccompanied gentlemen should never go."

"We went to a club."

"What sort of a club?" The reputable clubs gentlemen frequented were in the most fashionable neighborhoods, hardly dangerous territory.

"Exclusive gaming establishment. I was set upon walking home."

Emily thought he had bigger holes in his story than in his stockings. Going gaming with Phil, the least likely gentleman to go gaming on the sly or to spend the small hours of the night apart from his wife.

"Was Lady Ravenhurst there?" Her voice sounded small to her.

Lynley choked a little on the ale and recovered. "She was." He set the tankard aside. "Do you disapprove?"

It was not the question Emily expected. Lynley sat unmoving, his gaze fixed on his feet in the ruined stockings, waiting for her judgment. "Like your aunt, you mean?"

"Yes."

"No." She meant it. What she liked about him were the outrageous, impulsive things he did without regard to opinion. Well, that, and his person. He was a very...presentable gentleman. And he seemed in need of...a sympathetic touch. She jumped up and strode to the window.

"But I want to know why you engaged yourself to me in the midst of doing whatever it is you really came to London to do. What's my part in all this?"

"Ah," he said.

"Need time to collect your thoughts?" she asked. She took hold of the drapery cord and wound it around her hand. The idea that he was some sort of spy had taken hold of her mind. He'd dismissed the suggestion before, but now she meant to press him. "You are pursuing something? What? Missing government papers? Isn't that a job for"—she yanked the cord, sending a flood of bright light into the room—"a Runner or an agent or what, a spy?"

She stood blinking in the eye-watering sunlight, trying to disentangle the cord around her fingers, when she felt him come up behind her. He took hold of her shoulders and turned her to face him, pulling her back toward the sofa. She shook her arm to free it of the cord and stumbled, and his arms came around her, and they tumbled down onto the sofa. He winced, but he didn't let go.

She lay sprawled on top of him in a most unladylike awkwardness, her ear pressed to his beating heart, her legs tangled with his. She should push away, but his hand cupped her head and held her still. Under the thin lawn of his shirt, muscle and bone swelled and dipped. She rested her palm against his ribs and spread her fingers. He flinched even from her light touch.

"I have no lover's interest in Lady Ravenhurst," he said. His voice cracked as he spoke.

Emily lifted her head to meet his gaze, and tried to read the expression in his dark eyes.

* * * *

For a moment Lynley thought she might kiss him. His head swam with the scent of her, a piercing sweetness like the walled gardens of Jerez at night. Then he recognized the energy pulsing in her.

"You're thinking," he accused.

"Of course, I am. If you are not mooning over Lady Ravenhurst, then truly you are doing something else."

While his body absorbed with every nerve ending the sweet sensation of Emily Radstock lying upon him, apparently she was unaffected. "What if I can't tell you what that something is?"

A little furrow appeared between her brows. "Then how am I to help you?"

"Are you going to help?"

"Haven't I already? Your first scheme would never have succeeded without the distraction I provided." She lifted her hand from his ribs. "Help me up. I don't want to inflict any more damage on your person."

He put his hands to her waist and shifted her to a spot on the sofa beside him. She jumped up at once.

"Saline draft?"

He accepted the cup she offered, frowned at it, and tossed it down. She was smart. She knew London society more intimately than he did. And she was not faint of heart. "What are you willing to do to help?"

"Do you mean like leaping from a battlement or hiding with a dead man in his shroud?" She took the seat facing him. Her insubstantial gown was made of muslin trimmed with ribbon as green and golden as her eyes. He could not look away from the merry gleam of relish in those eyes.

"More like observing closely, listening to talk that you're not meant to hear, and creating distractions."

"No visits to noxious prisons or encounters with armed villains?" she asked.

"I can't promise." Maybe the saline solution was working. The day seemed brighter and his aches less noticeable.

"What *can* you tell me?"

"A guest at Lady Ravenhurst's party left with some gloves in his pocket, the gloves in which I found one of Lord Ravenhurst's missing papers. That guest went directly to the club where Phil and I went last night."

"So you went to see the place?"

"To see who meets whom there."

"You think someone from fashionable society is guilty of giving away British information? To whom?"

"Russian agents. There was a fellow, a Count Malikov. Did you ever meet him?"

"Of course. He went everywhere. He was too perfectly amiable for me. I thought he must be the sort who would stab you in the back if he saw a chance."

"He was. He also had a group of informants feeding him documents, some of whom apparently remain active."

"Where is Malikov now?"

"In a cell. Not talking, apparently. Waiting for his government to extricate him."

"So, if someone has stolen papers for Malikov, what does he do?"

"Gets desperate. Tries to find another taker for the papers. Makes a mistake."

She fell silent, studying the items on the tray. "A person with stolen papers can't exactly hawk them like a pie seller with his cart. You've already thought of that, haven't you?"

He nodded. "The holder of the papers is likely to go where he might be approached by someone who wants them, someone in the spy ring who has remained in the background so far, letting Malikov be known, but keeping his own identity hidden."

"But in London that could be anywhere. The park, a club, a party..." A thought seemed to strike her. She stood abruptly and walked to the window, staring out at the street. He waited for her to speak. "So you engaged yourself to me so that you could be in all those places, looking about, without anyone suspecting you of being a...spy."

The day had advanced. There was enough noise from the street, the clatter of carriages and hooves and the shouts of passersby to make it hard to catch the tone of her voice. He stood carefully, reminding himself that nothing had changed in two days. She was a delightful armful, but he had no interest in women who dreamed of happily ever after. The point of the speech he'd overheard her make in this room was that she did not really want to marry. She'd amused him with her fierceness, and he'd sympathized with her desire not to be managed by her relations. The engagement was made to suit them both. And it still could. If he let her in on the work, maybe he would find himself less distracted by her.

He came up behind her and rested his hands on her shoulders. "And now," he said, "we'll catch a spy together."

She turned and faced him, stepping back from his light hold on her shoulders. "As...partners," she said.

"Partners," he replied. Looking into the bright sun, he could not read her expression.

She stepped around him. He extended a hand, but she was already out of reach. "Good. I'll look at my cards of invitation. I think our next event must be a large party."

"Em—"

She opened the door, and there stood Phil, looking from one to the other of them.

"Oh, hello, Em," he said. "Roz is up. Did you come to see her?"

"Yes," she said, and was gone.

Chapter Ten

There is an ancient duty of hospitality that falls on those members of society blessed by fortune with large estates and grand edifices. Does Lady Castlewood possess a ballroom sufficiently large that three dozen couples or more may stand up at a time? Inevitably, Lady Castlewood feels her duty to send cards of invitation. Perhaps, over time, her ball becomes one of the highlights of the Season, anticipated by all. While this writer advises the husband hunter not to disdain the small dinner party, should the husband hunter receive an invitation to Lady Castlewood's ball, there can be only one response. Go!

—*The Husband Hunter's Guide to London*

Emily found Roz sitting up in bed in a pretty rose silk wrapper, sipping her morning chocolate, her black and white spaniel curled at her feet, everything cozy and soft. The dog thumped her tail on the blue coverlet in greeting, and Emily rubbed the silky ears.

Roz was just what Emily's spirits needed after her conversation with Lynley had brought her back to earth with a jarring bump. "You look very pretty," she told her sister.

Roz's expression turned wistful. "Thank you. One doesn't feel quite pretty, you know. How was the opera, Em?"

"You would have liked it, Roz. The princess's attendants cavorted in harem pants throughout the evening."

Roz sighed. "I do miss dancing."

"Longing for a quadrille or a waltz?"

"I am. It's nearly time for Lady Vange's grand ball. I've gone every year since my come out until now."

"Lady Vange's party? I'd forgotten it." Emily had gone to the grand affair twice before she'd abandoned husband hunting. She and Roz thought so differently about large parties. "Isn't Lady Vange's son Lord Hazelwood, the one who was..."

"Disgraced and disinherited?" Roz nodded and put down her chocolate. "But I read in the papers that he's recently married a respectable girl, so perhaps his family will forgive him."

Emily lifted the chocolate tray from Roz's bed and sank into a soft blue velvet armchair. She did not remember seeing the Vange invitation in the cards at home, but she would look. "It's a big party, isn't it?" Exactly the sort of affair she had avoided for years, but it would be the perfect event for spy hunting.

"Quite. Near four hundred guests. The dancing starts at eleven, and the supper goes on from two to near morning, with seating for sixty guests at a time. You and Lynley could go if he—" She broke off.

"You needn't conceal anything from me, Roz. I saw him this morning. He seems to be more or less in one piece, thanks to Phil apparently."

"I'm glad. Phil felt there was something wrong about that club. That's why he went back."

Emily glanced round the room decorated with her sister's usual blue and gold touches, but there were signs of Phil, too, in the dark, masculine wood of a pair of dressers and in a painting of horses and dogs gathering on a hunt morning. It was a shared space of two lives blended, not like the partnership to which she and Lynley had agreed.

"Em?" Roz recalled her to the present. "Are you sure you want to go on with your engagement?"

Emily managed a nod. "Why do you ask?"

"You look so serious is all."

"Me? Serious? Never. You are the one who is seriously missing dancing and feeling that you've lost your prettiness. I should be the concerned sister."

"I do miss going about. There is such a round of paying calls when one first marries. I suppose I got in the habit of it, and now...now I wait for people to call on me. I don't blame them for not coming, of course. I seem unable to speak of anything except the baby, as if no other subject exists. I'm sure most people would rather talk of other things."

"Roz, everyone has a favorite subject. Papa will talk for hours of porticoes, pillars, and staircases if you let him, and who is that young man who only speaks of his dogs?"

"Oh, Eversley."

"Don't be so hard on yourself. You've not stopped going out, have you?"

"Phil takes me for drives, and we walk a little, out of the way of everyone's notice. I look rather like your beloved Chunee."

"You do not."

Roz nodded solemnly. "I do. My gowns are tents as I refuse to wear those stays Doctor Collins recommends that put a squeeze on the baby."

"Very sensible of you, but could you not wear one of Mama's old high-waisted gowns?"

"Or stay home and wait for the Miss Throckmortons of the world to visit me." She cast Emily a questioning look.

"It is Miss Throckmorton, I take it, who reports my every misstep?"

Roz nodded. "Did you really dangle your ring for everyone in the park?"

"I did, but oh, Roz, it was only..."

"A little bit shocking?" Roz plucked at the blue coverlet. "Do you think it would be fun to be an opera dancer?"

"Fun? I should think it must be a most uncertain and very brief career."

"But a career. I think that if I didn't have Phil, I would like to be an opera dancer. You know, to be *doing* something."

"Roz, you *are* doing something. You are making a child."

"It's just that being on my own so much, I realize that I've never done anything shocking, and now I probably never will."

"That's because you are a woman of calm good sense. Besides, you may grow up to be as outrageous as your elder sister."

Roz laughed. "You are not so terribly outrageous, Em. Nothing like Lady Wingfield."

"Did Miss Throckmorton report on her, too?"

Roz nodded. "Lady Wingfield invited everyone to see her four-poster bed. Each of the posts is a gilt statue of Hercules with all his male parts displayed."

Emily laughed. "Then you are doomed to respectability, Roz. With your taste in furniture, you'll never get yourself talked of that way."

Roz laughed and threw off her coverlet. "Thank you, Em, you've cheered me."

Emily stood. She was the one who should be doing the thanking. Fifteen minutes of her sister's company had lifted her spirits. If her engagement had seemed briefly real, she had remembered in time that it was merely part of her scheme to take charge of her life. "Roz, if you want something to do, would you consider giving a small dinner for Lynley and me? For a few close friends."

"Of course, and soon." Roz gently cupped her round middle, holding her unborn child.

Chapter Eleven

In the mind of a young person, convention appears as the fossilized remains of a former age, as absurd as powdered wigs and beauty patches. Convention, our modern miss declares, is the enemy of feeling and worthy only of contempt. This writer must disagree. The conventions of a fourteen-week Season are no more to be disdained than the conventions of the fourteen-line sonnet. Like the genius of our island, the husband hunter must express depth of feeling and true sincerity within the bounds of convention.

—*The Husband Hunter's Guide to London*

Emily tried to banish thoughts of Lynley as she prepared to mount Circe for a morning ride, but a picture of him waking on that green sofa intruded. She worked to imagine him elsewhere in some sedate, gentlemanly set of rooms, but the effort led to an image of him lying sealed in an envelope of warm sheets, a valet hovering solicitously near, waiting to minister to his every need. She told herself with some satisfaction that his first utterance this morning would likely be a groan.

The clop of hooves on the cobbles interrupted the thought, and she glanced away from Circe. There was Lynley on a handsome chestnut with a white blaze from forehead to nose.

"Why are you here?" She blinked at the vision of him, the perfectly turned-out gentleman from his polished top boots and buff riding breeches to the slight tilt of his hat.

"To get started on our...case," he answered.

She blinked again. He was there. Real. No injuries apparent except for the yellowing bruise on his jaw above the white linen of his neckcloth. "You'll have to settle for the tamest walk."

"Not a gallop?"

"You don't think I gallop in the park? It would be against all propriety."

He grinned at her and dismounted. "You ride at this hour precisely to defy propriety. In any case, your horse will tell the truth of your morning rides, if you won't."

He was right. Circe would react to any deviation in their familiar routine, and he would notice. Her fiancé was no imbecile after all.

"Shall we?" he asked. He stepped to her side, and his hands formed a pocket. It was no more than any groom would do for a lady. She gathered her skirts and gave him her foot. Just that, her foot nestled in his hands, sent a bolt of warmth through her that settled low in her belly. She gathered her wits. One spring from her, and he lifted her easily. It was a quick thing, a few seconds in the air before her bottom met the saddle and her legs found their usual positions hooked around the sidesaddle's double pommel. Her feet searched for the stirrups, found them, and slid securely into place.

"I thought you had a black horse," she said, squaring her shoulders and arranging her skirts, covering a little tremor in her nerves that really must be from the cold.

He stood looking up at her, one hand on Circe's neck, as if his mind had wandered down some side path and left him standing there. The horses' nostrils streamed vapor in the cool air of the April morning. Circe tossed her head at the delay, and Lynley seemed to come back to himself.

"At home," he said as if there had been no gap in the conversation. "This fellow is one of Phil's." He remounted and gave the chestnut's neck a pat. Obviously, an understanding already existed between them.

They walked the horses through the quiet streets to the park. In Emily's ears the horses' hooves struck loud enough against the stones to wake even those Londoners who had only just sought their beds after the night's round of society gatherings. In the sleeping houses the servants would be up and about but pay them no heed. On the street a cart clattered by in a brief burst of sound, the driver intent on his own errand.

Emily resisted the impulse to hurry. Once or twice she peeked to see whether she could detect a grimace on his face. Even a walking pace would jar Lynley's injuries. They entered the park by the northern gate and wound their way down to Emily's favorite bridle path. The softer ground of the path turned the horses' hoofbeats to muffled thuds in keeping with the stillness of the hour. When Circe began to fidget at the slow pace, eager

for her morning release of spirits and energy, Emily risked a direct look
a Lynley. He grinned back.

"Now we canter?" he asked. "Down and back?"

Emily glanced down the empty path and nodded, and he was off. Circe
needed no coaxing to fly after the chestnut. The mist parted, trees blurred
into a pale green curtain, dirt flew up under Circe's belly. The park became
a fairy park, green and enchanted, where no faces frowned, no voices
intruded, as girl and horse flew by. Emily let herself get lost in the familiar
pleasure of it, only surprised to discover Lynley and the chestnut falling
into step beside them, the horses running like a matched pair.

At the far end of the path they wheeled and pulled up, and Lynley turned
to her, an eyebrow quirked, a question in his glance. He knew what she
and Circe wanted. Emily nodded and gave Circe her head, and off they
went. It was mad, of course, even at such an hour, but Emily felt that she
and Circe could go on forever.

Abruptly, Lynley caught Circe's bridle straps and pulled the horses to
a halt. Emily turned to complain, when she saw an elderly couple coming
their way at a sedate pace.

Lynley bowed to them as they passed. "Good morning," he said. "Please
forgive poor Miss Radstock. Her horse ran away with her. So lucky I could
be of assistance." He assumed his amiable idiot voice.

Emily fixed a polite smile on her lips.

Once the elderly riders were out of earshot, he released Circe's bridle.

"How are your ribs?" she asked him, conscious of the broken harmony of
the moment before. They had been united briefly in that other park where
Emily was most herself. Now they were back in London, where ladies did
not gallop and gentlemen always took charge.

"Shaken," he said through tight lips.

She shook her head. "You insisted."

"I did. Now I insist that you make it worth my while."

"What?" She spun toward him, and Circe danced a little.

"Let's make a plan to catch a spy," he said, his face all innocence.

"Oh, of course."

"I have the guest list from Lady Ravenhurst's party. I thought we might...
study it. Over breakfast."

"You're inviting yourself to breakfast?"

He shrugged. "You wanted to catch a spy."

* * * *

Though she knew in her head that she would find Lynley sitting at her mother's breakfast table when she returned from changing her habit, his presence nevertheless sent a shock through her. He sat on the far side of the table, looking with undivided attention at a paper list, a cup of steaming coffee and a plate of an astonishing amount of food in front of him. As always, he dominated the space with his height and ease of manner.

He looked up briefly. "We start with Archer. Phil says he's part of a fast set into gaming, sports, and women. Do you know any of his connections?"

Emily turned immediately to the sideboard. "Archer?" she asked, looking at the dishes of eggs and meat, toast and buns.

She set her plate at her usual place, where she'd sat alone for so long, looking out the window at the square, finding amusement in the comings and goings of her neighbors. Now he was her view.

He turned the list around and shoved it across the table for her to look at it. "Archer's the fellow who carried off the gloves last night."

Emily nodded and regarded the items on her plate, trying to see if anything looked appealing. Lynley's presence interfered with her appetite.

"I have to say that looking at these names, it's hard to imagine a spy in the group."

"Anyone with diplomatic ties or foreign interests?"

Emily shook her head. She recognized most of the names. They were old London families with unblemished reputations. Even Archer, though she did not know the young man, had an older married sister who was the epitome of respectability. No one on the list appeared to be the sort who had stolen confidential government documents to sell to Russian spies.

"Anyone with embarrassing vices that an unscrupulous person might threaten to expose?"

"Not that I know of. Lady Derwent is known for her excellent dinners. Mrs. Gilbey-Wilkes is extraordinarily long-winded, and Lord Illingworth must be right on every debatable point, but such faults will not make them spies."

"Then, we are back to Archer."

Emily shook her head. "We start with Lady Ravenhurst, I think," she said, deciding she could handle a bite of toast.

He regarded his plate. "Why?"

"Because she's at the center." She took the saucer from under her dish of tea and put her finger in the center. "And because one always pays morning calls to thank a hostess for her hospitality. We want to see how she appears, whether she is in distress over the events of the other evening, and most importantly, we want to see who leaves her cards. They will all be displayed in the entry." She drew her finger around the rim of the saucer.

For a moment he said nothing, just watched the movement of her finger. Then he lifted his gaze to hers. She could not fathom his expression.

A week earlier she had sat in the same place, at the same table, with her father, who had barely acknowledged her presence. Her heart gave a funny skip under Lynley's regard. She changed the subject. "I do know Archer's older sister, Beatrix. She's married with two small children. I can pay her a visit."

"Good."

"Of course, it might be awkward to begin a series of inquiries about the scrapes into which her brother has fallen."

He nodded and addressed his attention to the eggs and bacon on his plate, as if, like her father, he'd forgotten she was there.

"You really don't know London protocol, do you?"

"I don't. Hence, our partnership."

"Let me tell you," she said, "a little of how it works."

"Enlighten me." He dug into his eggs as if she had no influence on his nerves or appetite in any way. She looked at her plate. Why should her appetite suffer while his clearly remained unimpaired?

Her toast was too dry, and she reached for a pot of marmalade. "It's all in the timing, and in the use of one's calling cards. You don't have cards, do you?"

"I do." More of his eggs disappeared.

"With a London address?"

"Alas, no."

"Should we have some cards printed? Sir Ajax Lynley, Baronet, of Lord Woodford's green and peony damask sofa."

"Again, I bow to your superior knowledge of polite society, but I doubt that address would suit sticklers like my aunt."

"Apparently, you don't want anyone, including your fiancée, to know where to find you."

He didn't deny it. "In any case, you will use your own cards when you make these calls." He put down his fork, his plate empty. Marmalade dripped from the toast in her hand.

"Well, then, let's consider the timing."

"Let's," he agreed.

"I must call on Lady Ravenhurst at her next at-home day. The best time will be as her first visitors are leaving. With a little bit of care I may contrive a few minutes alone with her. On the other hand, politeness dictates that with Archer's sister I must be among the earliest visitors, and cannot count on any private conference."

"Fair enough. I'll look forward to your findings." He put his napkin on the table, and stood. "If you'll pardon me, I'll be off." He offered a bow and strolled toward the door.

A suspicion hit her at his easy acceptance of their plan. "What will you be doing?"

"Me?" He halted, his hand on the knob. "I thought I'd follow Phil round to his club."

"Wait. That's not your plan." Emily scrambled up from her chair.

"It's not?"

Emily closed the gap between them, tempted to jab him in his bruised ribs. "You may have fooled your aunt with that act, but it doesn't fool me."

"I never fooled my aunt. She never doubted that I was on the path to ruin and would end in hell."

The momentary glimpse into his unhappy boyhood stopped her.

He looked amused at her confusion. "You don't think I should go to Phil's club?"

"I know that's not your plan." Then she got it. "You're going to see that Russian in jail, aren't you?"

His expression sobered at once. "Where he's being kept is no place for a lady. And the chances of his saying anything are very little."

"Nevertheless, if we are partners in this enterprise, you'll take me with you." She held up her hand with its extravagant ring. "My love."

Chapter Twelve

It must be acknowledged that the husband hunter will find villains enough in London, though they will hardly be of the sort she encounters in her favorite novel. She is unlikely to meet dangerous brigands or daring pirates, but she will inevitably meet the careless, the indifferent, the self-concerned, and even the heartless among her male and female acquaintance in the great metropolis. Backstabbing, gossip, and betrayal are their weapons, and they are quite as capable of causing misery as any villain who would pursue the husband hunter across oceans and down American rivers to achieve his wicked ends.

—*The Husband Hunter's Guide to London*

Lynley ducked to enter the office of the governor's house of the prison. In the little room a pair of clerks bent over their work behind a wainscoted partition. It might have been the anteroom of any ordinary business except for the turnkey at the door and the open ledger in which visitors were to inscribe their names and the name of the prisoner they wished to visit.

The servant who examined their credentials offered Emily a pen. The ruse they'd invented for the visit depended on her, and she'd been the one to think of it. Count Malikov was being kept in one of the cells for condemned men, under an assumed name. He mixed with no one.

As far as prison officials knew, the man they had in custody was Thomas Culley, who had killed a man during a housebreaking. This afternoon Emily was to be his distraught wife, desperate to take leave of him before the Recorder's report would fix his fate and he would move toward his inevitable end.

She was dressed in fine black wool and wore a hat with a black veil as well. She looked as little like her lively self as it was possible for her to look. She carried a square of linen in her hand, which she pressed occasionally to her eyes. A tremor ran through her as she signed the book. She scarcely glanced Lynley's way, though she leaned on his arm as they waited for the chaperone who would accompany her. Lynley could sense her impatience to get on with it.

The chaperone arrived, a clerical-looking man in black.

"Mrs. Culley?" he asked.

She nodded.

"You are allowed a quarter hour only. You will speak through the grate. A guard will be in the space between you and the prisoner. Do you understand?"

She nodded again.

"Come along then, ma'am." The chaperone nodded to the turnkey, who opened the office door.

They stepped into the lodge with its sets of heavy shackles on the wall and faced an oaken gate, bound with iron and studded with nails. The turnkey opened the gate and motioned for Emily and her chaperone to pass through. For a brief instant Lynley could see a narrow stone passage that seemed to dead-end in a turning.

"Remain 'ere, sir," the turnkey said.

The gate closed on her, and Lynley's heart contracted briefly. She was smart. She was cool under fire. She'd be fine. They had studied the layout of the prison. He knew where the narrow passage would take her, and where she would descend to the ward of cells for the condemned. He looked at his watch. She would return in half an hour. He could wait.

In Jerez it would be the siesta hour. There, Lynley had learned how to stretch out on any surface and summon sleep to pass the long, indolent afternoons before he could return to his horses and his work. He had learned that one's impatience could not hurry the clock along, but the prison lodge held no sofa, not even a bench for waiting out the time. The irons on the walls offered no comforting distraction.

He returned to the office where she had signed the book. The clerks continued their work without looking up, the scratching of their pens purposeful and regular. Nothing on the shelves drew his notice. Nothing on the walls engaged his attention. An unfamiliar restlessness consumed him. The room permitted no more than two strides in either direction. He set himself a steady pace. He was not a man to imagine trouble, so it made no sense that his mind should now count the gates she would pass through. One of the clerks looked up. "Sir, do ye mind? Can ye settle?"

Lynley nodded. He turned to the guest book on the table and read the page she'd signed. He'd not seen her writing before, neat, clear, confident, and boldly feminine in its curving lines and small flourishes. He read through the names of visitors. The prison had had a busy day. Mr. Campion, Mr. Hassell, Mr. Clark, and Mr. Perry had all had visitors. Lynley flipped to the previous page in the book, letting his finger pass down the page. Then he stopped cold on an entry that should not have been there. Thomas Culley, a fiction, a man whose existence should not be known to anyone outside the inner circle of the Foreign Office, had had a visitor at noon.

Lynley pounded on the office door. He had to get to her.

* * * *

Emily followed the turnkey through the heavy oak door, down a narrow turning passageway, already gloomy, made gloomier by the veil on her hat. At each turning there was another gate or grate to be unlocked, opened, and relocked again after they passed through, with a jarring clang of metal. Each swing of one of the heavy doors disturbed the stale air of decay in the passage, reminding Emily of her fear for Arthur Broome in that other jail, that he would succumb to one of the miasma-borne fevers of London's prisons.

Emily enjoyed the pleasure of a maze in a country garden, lost in the turnings of high, dense hedges of yew or boxwood. But in a maze, however hemmed in, one could look up at blue sky and hear the voices of others playing the game. Here she kept her gaze on the back of the turnkey in front of her, not on the crypt-like stone ceiling above her. Lynley would have to duck at every turn.

She was conscious of her dependence on the two men with her, silent and yet censorious. They believed her to be the wife of a dangerous felon. In them there was no pity for the man she hoped to see, and none for his wife, or pretended wife. At the end of several turnings, one more heavy iron grate opened on an obscure curving staircase. Here the pestilential smell made her gag briefly and hold her bit of linen to her mouth and nose.

"Mind yer step, ma'am," the turnkey said.

Emily lifted her skirts and put a gloved hand to the rough wall to steady herself as they descended. At the bottom of a flight of steps a charcoal stove cast a lurid light along a passage with three cells, each with a massive door. The turnkey directed her the other way, to a narrow cell like a dog's kennel. "Wait here, ma'am," he said.

Emily stepped inside. At shoulder height in one of the sides of the cell was a grate onto a space a little more than a yard wide. Emily looked across the gap that was to separate her from the man she came to see. Her clerical-looking chaperone stayed in the passage, blocking her exit. There was nowhere to look but straight ahead at a grate opposite.

When they brought Malikov from his cell, he would be no more than a shadowy figure opposite. The guard would stand in the space between them.

Emily took a steadying breath. She and Lynley had rehearsed this part. She knew what she was to say, how she was to tell the Russian that it was still possible that he could be released from this place, that he had only to tell the truth about his confederates in crime for the government to arrange for him to be removed from these dreadful circumstances. *A name frees you*, she would say.

It was what a wife might say in such circumstances, but it was also, at the same time, a message to a spy about how he might bargain for his freedom with the British government.

She clasped her gloved hands together, reminding herself that Malikov was no Arthur Broome, no kind man in jail for his principles, but rather a ruthless spy, willing to endanger and betray anyone for his country's advantage. The risk was that he could unmask her. He could deny her as his wife. She would be at the mercy of the turnkey and her chaperone, with more than a dozen locked gates between her and Lynley.

Running steps and jangling keys interrupted her thoughts. Metal clanged. Hurried steps went up the staircase. Her chaperone called out "What's happened, man?" and ran down the passage. She stepped out of the little cell, looking toward the great oaken door that hung open. Her chaperone waved her back.

Emily stopped. From above more footsteps pounded down the stairs. Two armed guards rushed to the open cell door.

The turnkey reappeared, his arms outstretched to contain her. "You. Stay where you are," he hissed at her.

He looked over his shoulder at one of the guards, who nodded to him from the cell door, and Emily darted forward under his outstretched arm. "What's happened? Something's wrong with my husband. I must see him."

"Never ye mind, ma'am," said the chaperone, reaching for her arm.

Emily shook him off. "Let me see him. Oh, I must see him." She halted, catching hold of the cell doorjamb.

Malikov lay on the stones in the dark, narrow cell reeking of its chamber pot. He had apparently dropped to his knees and pitched forward, his face turned to the side, one arm outstretched across the floor, the wrist enclosed in iron.

Emily knelt at his side. His teeth had fixed in a rigid grin. His unseeing eyes stared. She closed them and huddled over the body, her mind working furiously. He was dead because the government had failed to protect him. Someone beside themselves had gained the secret of his identity. There must be some clue she could give to Lynley.

"Now see here, ma'am. It's not permitted." The turnkey held a lantern up over the scene. In its light a thin rivulet of sparkling liquid ran from Malikov's outstretched fingers to pool under a narrow iron bench attached to the wall. Emily's gaze followed the faint glitter to a fallen metal cup. She sniffed as if in grief and inhaled a familiar sour smell. Perhaps the last thing Malikov had done in life was to drink his beer allowance.

"Guards!" the turnkey shouted.

Rough hands pulled at her shoulders. She went limp, clinging to Malikov's hand. His fingers were wet. The turnkey swore. The lantern swung above her head, and under the dead man's hand, Emily read his last word written on the stones in spilled beer.

"Unhand Mrs. Culley." The snapped command came from Lynley. The rough hands immediately released her.

Emily raised herself up from the corpse. "Brother," she cried.

He pulled her to her feet and held her close to his side, leaning down to whisper in her ear. "If you never fainted in your life, now would be good time to start."

"Oh my poor husband," she wailed. "Oh, I feel—" She broke off and let herself slump in Lynley's arms.

"Let me remove my sister from this noxious cell," Lynley said. "And you can get on with your business."

* * * *

In the carriage outside the prison Lynley felt he could breathe again. He had a strong desire to shake his companion, and an equally strong desire to crush her to him and not let go. She had done what a man would have done. She had rushed to the dead man and examined the scene, apparently indifferent to the danger of being unmasked as an imposter.

Every gate that had to be opened for them to pass had been a trial. Every place where he'd had to stoop and squeeze in the narrow passage had tested him. He had been mistaken in thinking that his aunt made Lyndale Abbey a prison. Confinement to the abbey, with its gloomy rooms full of painted saints frowning down from the walls, was freedom compared with a genuine English prison. He had to report to Goldsworthy as quickly as he could, but first he needed to get Emily Radstock away from danger.

She knew something. Excitement still coursed through her at the adventure she'd had. Her body shook with it.

"Lynley, he was murdered," she said.

"I gathered. Did you see a wound?"

She shook her head. "When he fell, he must have had a cup of beer in his hand. I could smell it on the stones. The cup rolled under the bench."

"Poisoned then?"

"How could it be done unless someone on the inside was in on it?"

Lynley considered the likely candidates. "Malikov had a visitor earlier today. Easy enough to bribe a guard to offer the prisoner a ration of beer with an extra something in it."

"Who? Who wanted him dead?" She lifted the veil on her hat, her eyes large and bright with adventure and indignation.

"The name in the book is Mr. Isaiah Peach." Lynley had recognized the message in the name at once.

"The visitor, whoever he was, must have known Malikov's true identity. Even so, the turnkey and chaperone were there, and no visitor would be admitted to the cell, nor could he offer anything to Malikov through the grates with a guard standing between them."

Lynley understood how the thing could be done. Peach's role, whoever he was, had been to distract the prisoner. "Malikov would have been removed from his cell long enough for another guard to put something in his beer."

"Lynley, there's something else," she said.

"What?"

"Malikov tried to write something in the spilled beer. A name, I imagine. There were only three letters—Z-O-V. Do you think Zov was Mr. Peach's real name?"

"No." Lynley doubted the visitor had been Russian. More likely Isaiah Peach was a local hired to do the job.

Lynley didn't like it. Malikov had been murdered for knowing things. Even his refusal to betray his fellow spies to the English had not saved him. Now Lynley had involved Emily in the case. Now Emily knew things she ought not to know.

"You're frowning. What?" she asked.

He reached for her and pulled her onto his lap. He simply had to hold her for a few minutes. "I want you out of these clothes," he said.

"Lynley!" She twisted to look at him, her elbow catching him in his bruised ribs. "I appreciate that we've had a trying afternoon, but there's no reason to lose your head. We're on Fleet Street in a moving carriage with a good part of the population of London passing by."

He took hold of her dangerous elbows. As soon as he'd said it, he realized that he'd meant just what she thought, but it would not do to admit it.

"I meant," he said, "that your skirts have been in contact with who knows what offensive, possibly poisonous substances. I think you should burn this dress."

"Oh, of course. Good thought." She softened and leaned against him. "I must thank you for coming into the cell at just that moment. I feared the guards would detain me. We make a good team."

He said nothing. He tucked her head under his chin and closed his arms around her. A glaring flaw in agreeing to their partnership now became apparent. As his partner, she, too, would encounter danger. He could lose her, not in the way he expected, at the end of their partnership, but in a way he didn't care to think of at all. He resolved to keep their partnership to ballrooms and drawing rooms. He would see to it that from now on he faced villains alone.

Chapter Thirteen

With very little effort the husband hunter can, in fact, acquire a husband in her first Season, as long as she is not too nice in her requirements. The world will be quite satisfied to see her matched with a respectable gentleman of means and unexceptional appearance. A few smiles, a little gratitude for his notice, and a willing acceptance of his addresses will do the trick. The banns may be called, the bride cake ordered, and the guests notified.

The husband hunter who refuses to accept such fleeting success, the triumph of which is over on the wedding day itself, must be patient indeed. In the midst of the Season's gaiety, surrounded by gentlemen with all the charm of looks and manners to recommend them, she must wait for that rare gentleman who awakens her deepest instincts, the very instincts which guide the way she lives her life. With him she will risk the unthinkable. To him only may she give an unequivocal yes! that makes both tremble with joy.

—*The Husband Hunter's Guide to London*

Goldsworthy met Lynley's announcement of Malikov's death with a shake of his great mangy russet locks, like a lion disturbed over a fresh kill. He pushed up from the huge desk faster than Lynley imagined a man of his size could move, and strode to pull the bell.

"He had a visitor, you say?"

"One Isaiah Peach. This morning. Hardly a subtle message."

"And you arrived when?"

"This afternoon around one."

"Did you see the body? What happened?"

"I suspect poison. My guess is that Peach distracted Malikov, while one of the guards brought him doctored beer."

There was a knock on the door, and at Goldsworthy's answer, Nate Wilde entered.

"Wilde, lad. Need you to go at once to find your old Bow Street friend Will Jones. A suspicious death at the prison needs to be investigated. Get Jones on the scene quick as you can, before the governor tries to cover everything up."

"Yes, sir," Wilde answered. He took off at a run.

Goldsworthy frowned down at his enormous desk. "They'll say it's jail fever."

"If you don't mind my saying so, sir, the Foreign Office appears to leak like a sieve."

"I do mind your saying so, lad, damn ye, but you're right. That's why we need you to find out who's taking papers."

Goldsworthy had revealed Malikov's false name and his location only because the Foreign Office had so far failed to find the remaining members of the Russian spy ring.

"Malikov managed to write a message in the spilled beer. The word *Zov.* Mean anything, sir?"

"Zovsky, another suspected Russian agent. He generally operates out of Paris."

"You don't think Zovsky was Peach?"

"I doubt it. Zovsky's too cagey. They all are, blast them. He'd hire someone. This fellow Peach would not know the plan or the target. He'd just play his part and collect some coin." Goldsworthy crossed from his desk to study one of the maps of London on the office wall.

Lynley stood beside the big man. "If Peach is from London, he'll have a corner or a public house where he can be found."

Goldsworthy tapped the map with a thick finger in three spots around the prison. "Exactly so, lad. And Wilde will likely find him soon enough with a little help from our friend Jones, unless Peach has taken himself out of London, which he might do when he hears what happened."

He turned to Lynley. "I don't want you to tip your hand, now, lad. It's best that the other side thinks of you only as a young fool in love. Back to the ballrooms and drawing rooms you go."

Lynley nodded. He had no problem with that. A ballroom or a park in full view of the fashionable half of London was exactly where he wanted Emily Radstock to be. Well, almost where he wanted her to be.

* * * *

The morning after their prison adventure Emily received two messages, one from Lynley, and one from her mother.

My dear Emily, her mother wrote.

Nurse and I do our best to keep your grandmother comfortable. She sits in the sun most mornings, takes some nourishment, and derives great comfort from the signs of spring outside her window, the first bluebells and the blackthorn in blossom. I'm sorry, my dear girl, that I must be away from you at this time. I realize that you must be longing for a mother's advice and counsel as you face the many decisions on which your happy day depends. I am glad to hear that Roz will host a party in your honor. Very proper. Is it true that your ring is the size of an acorn?

Your affectionate mother.

Lynley's note said he would see her after she made the morning calls they'd planned. Emily did not know which note bothered her more. She wrote to her mother immediately, and contemplated sending Lynley a message directed to Roz's sofa, the only place she knew to look for him.

Clearly, Lynley had taken the information they'd gained together back to his spy colleagues, and just as clearly, he did not want her to have a direct encounter with England's enemies. He saw their roles as separate and not at all equal. Nevertheless, in the end she set out to pay the morning calls as they'd agreed.

She stood in Lady Ravenhurst's entry hall, studying two dozen cards on the silver salver. Earlier callers had filled her ladyship's drawing room, and the lady herself had circulated gaily among them. Still, as Emily drew on her gloves, she kept thinking that Lady Ravenhurst had been keenly disappointed in her company. Though she had turned eagerly to the door as each new guest was announced, at each arrival her face had betrayed a fleeting disappointment. She had plainly anticipated a visitor who never came. Emily gave the cards one more quick look, and turned to the footman at the door. Her carriage would be waiting.

Outside, it was not her father's coachman, but Lynley waiting for her, next to Phil's curricle.

Emily glanced down at the steps to cover her surprise. She had been thinking him elsewhere this morning, reporting to his mysterious employer or sleeping in his secret quarters, wherever they were. Even Phil claimed not to know.

"Hello," Lynley said and offered his hand to help her up into the vehicle. The day was fine, with the plane trees in flower and leaf in the square, and just the hint of a breeze. "Learn anything?"

"In a way, yes," she said. It was hard to put it into words, but she suspected that Lady Ravenhurst had a lover. Emily had heard no gossip linking the lady to another, but then Emily had been ignoring the fashionable world, absorbed in Chunee's death and Arthur Broome's arrest.

Returning to the more conventional activities of the Season made sense after their failed attempt to talk to Malikov. Her mother's letter, too, had been a reminder that Emily and Lynley needed to keep up the appearance of a courting couple. Only he and she knew that their courtship had stopped its forward progress. No barristers met to arrange settlements. Neither caterers nor clergymen had been notified. No guest lists had been drawn up or bride clothes ordered.

And yet Lynley had said, *I want you out of these clothes.* The idea haunted her. His words came to mind at the most awkward times, like now as he settled beside her in the curricle. Recalling his words made her clothes feel tight against her skin.

He gave his horses the order to walk on.

She stared ahead while he navigated the traffic around the square. She had understood that with those words he meant to express his concern for some contamination to her garments from the floor of Malikov's cell, but she had also understood, instantly, in that moment, with a clarity that had flooded her body in heat, that he meant it in a different, more direct way as well.

Her heart had been pounding with the thrill of their escape from the prison. It had been an escape. Someone in that small party of prison officials had permitted murder, and that someone would not want his actions examined. An entry in the register in the governor's office had tipped Lynley off before Emily, in the deepest recesses of the prison, had realized the danger. He had come for her, and she could only guess at how he had felt in the confined spaces of those passages and cells, where his head and shoulders could barely squeeze through. And so in the carriage, when they were free of the place, he had let a thought escape. He was a most provoking man. She certainly wasn't taking off her clothes while he wore all of his.

"Well?" he asked.

"Lady Ravenhurst was expecting someone who did not make an appearance. She had dozens of visitors, but no one gave her joy. I think we're looking for someone who wasn't there."

"Like Archer?" he asked.

"Possibly. It's not too late. I will call on his sister, if you'll take me there."

"It was my plan," he said. He wore the usual accouterments of a gentleman out for a drive—a black hat and tan gloves, a fawn driving coat and polished boots. Little of his person was visible except his face, and yet Emily felt his presence next to her, exerting some pull, stronger than old Newton's gravity itself.

She sat very straight and fixed her gaze on the horses' heads. "Did you learn anything more about Zov or Mr. Peach?"

"I did. Isaiah Peach is actually Isaiah Kydd of the Seven Dials. He's probably known to many of the guards, for he frequents a public house in Giltspur Street. Apparently, he's available for hire cheap, and his acquaintances say he's left London."

"And Zov?"

"Is a man named Zovsky, who operates in Paris, much as Malikov did in London." He paused. "My...sources doubt that Zovsky would come to London, as his appearance is known, and he would not risk being taken up in an inquiry."

Emily noticed the care he took to keep those sources confidential. Their partnership had its limits, which she would do well to remember. "So, we don't know how Malikov's identity got known, or who hired Peach, or how the poison, if it was poison, got into Malikov's drink."

Lynley laughed. "We don't, but remember what we want is the missing papers, and Malikov couldn't have taken them."

"Still, it's reasonable to think that the work of an informant in the Foreign Office is behind the murder as well as the missing papers."

"Congratulations, Em," he said. "You think very much like the man who is on the hunt for that leak. He wants to find any remaining members of Malikov's network."

Em! "And he expects us to do so?"

Lynley grinned at her and nodded.

At Beatrix Walsingham's Castle Street house, Emily handed the butler her card and was invited up at once to a pale green drawing room.

"Hello, Emily, how long has it been? I'm so glad you've come. I was in danger of eating all these cakes myself." Beatrix gestured to a tray of iced yellow cakes. "You must have news to tell, as you've become engaged at last, I hear. And your sister is to have a baby."

Emily smiled and took the seat offered. "My mother is thrilled," she said, explaining also that her mother was away, and remembering belatedly that Beatrix's mother had died unexpectedly not three years earlier. Before Beatrix's marriage to Walsingham, the two friends had compared notes on their mothers' efforts to get them married.

Beatrix was sympathetic as she poured tea, and Emily found it easy to fall into conversation with her old friend, as if they'd simply been interrupted for a few minutes instead of a few years. She told of Roz's desire to be an opera dancer and gave Beatrix the version of her engagement that she and Lynley had fashioned together.

Beatrix sighed at the conclusion of Emily's account. "Now, if only I could see my brother settled. With our parents gone, I feel he's been added to my care. Though he's of age, you know what young men are. I feel he needs a woman to steady him."

Emily reached for one of the little cakes. She had not expected such an opening to the very subject most near to their investigation. Pretending to be Thomas Culley's wife seemed less false than the charade she now played with her old friend. "Is there no one who's caught his eye?" she asked.

"I'm afraid not. Do you go to Lady Vange's ball?"

"Yes."

"You may see him there. I've tried to interest him in this Season's beauty, a girl named Allegra Walhouse. Do you know her?"

Emily shook her head.

"Well, he'll have none of the girl. I suppose I'm well served for my matchmaking efforts."

"I will keep an eye out, shall I, and report to you?" It was both a truth and a lie at once. She could easily report to Beatrix, but her first report would be to Lynley, a report he would take to his mysterious colleagues in the Foreign Office.

"Would you? I'm afraid Archer is in a bad crowd. He boasted to me that he won fifty guineas earlier this winter on a wager that a certain married lady would take a lover. You can imagine my shock, but he laughed at it and told me I have grown duller than dishwater."

In no time at all, the visit passed. Emily reached over to give her friend's hand a squeeze. By giving up on husband hunting, Emily had unintentionally separated herself from friends who did marry. "Before I go, I must know that you, yourself, are well and happy?"

Beatrix's smile reappeared. "I am. Fashionable people would laugh at me, I know, but I like motherhood. It may not be the thing to pay so much attention to one's babies, but I confess they fascinate me. They go so rapidly from knowing nothing of the world to speaking and counting and questioning everything."

"I'm glad to hear you say it. Would you call on Roz if you can? She's approaching her confinement, and it would do her good to hear you talk."

"Of course. She probably feels like your poor elephant."

"She does." Emily laughed.

"You see, I do keep up. I read your letter in the *Times*."

In parting they agreed to meet again and compare notes on their relations. Lynley stood on the flagway to assist Emily up into the curricle.

He turned the vehicle, and they headed back to Candover House.

"Tired of spying?" he asked.

"Am I so easily read?"

"Yesterday, there was danger and excitement. Today must seem tame."

"That's not it exactly. It's more the falseness of the thing. I did not feel so false pretending to be Mrs. Culley, as I do pretending an interest in my friends for the sake of gaining information from them."

"Did you gain any information?"

"Beatrix's brother Archer won fifty guineas earlier this winter on a wager that a certain married lady would take a lover."

"Lady Ravenhurst?"

"Beatrix didn't know, or didn't say, but Lady Ravenhurst is unhappy in her marriage." It struck Emily that one could be isolated in the midst of a great city, a city of a million people. The thread connecting the two women she'd visited had been loneliness. And now that she thought of it, Malikov had been lonely and isolated in death. And perhaps his loneliness had begun with his becoming a spy, with choosing to step out of the circle of genuine friendship, to become instead an observer and a manipulator, a keeper of information on others, rather than a man who exchanged the true thoughts and feelings on which attachments were founded.

"Lynley, if you were taken by the Russians, England would not send a man to silence you?"

"You think Malikov's government ordered him killed?"

"That's why he wrote Zovsky's name in the beer, isn't it?" The possibility troubled her. Malikov could not have been an entirely good man, but he had been loyal to his country, and his country had abandoned him in a foreign jail and, perhaps worse, had contrived to have him killed.

"Possibly, but Zovsky may have acted on his own to protect himself."

"It's just that—" Emily broke off. What she'd been about to say shocked her and was better left unsaid. She would not let errant thoughts just spill out, as he had.

"Just what?" he asked.

"I'm ready to go home," she said. She did not want to find Lynley lying cold and still in a pool of beer. What she wanted, and it had been strikingly clear to her in a flash, was Lynley lying naked in a great bed. "Perhaps our paper thief will reveal himself at Lady Vange's ball." She smiled up at Lynley with what she hoped was a sweetly docile expression.

Chapter Fourteen

There are those who would advise the husband hunter to conceal her intelligence from gentlemen who take an interest in her. In this writer's view, such advice is utterly misguided. Few qualities are as attractive or as misunderstood as genuine intelligence. In the future we may be able to name the several different forms that intelligence takes. At the present time, we may charitably interpret such wrong-headed advice to mean that the husband hunter should not attempt displays of pedantry. No one needs to know of her superior knowledge of languages or maps, scientific principles or moral abstracts. Rather she should confine herself to that display of attention which reveals her powers of observation and insight.

—*The Husband Hunter's Guide to London*

Emily thought it possible that not everyone in London had squeezed into Vange House. After all, Lady Vange's invitation was a coveted one. Guests had decked themselves out in glittering jewels and gold braid and had applied sufficient pomade and perfume to rival the sweeter scents of the potted orange trees and Cape jessamines that circled the great ballroom. If a spy had joined the throng, he could easily lose himself in the packed crowd.

Emily had believed, however, she was in no danger of losing Lynley, as his height made him unmistakable. In such a crush a lady could lose a glove, a fan, or an earring, but not a fiancé.

Of course, she'd been wrong. She had arrived with her father and Lynley, and could find neither. Now that the dancing was about to begin, she'd quite lost her fiancé, and was in danger of being spotted by Miss Throckmorton. Emily glanced round for an opening in the shoulder-to-shoulder throng of young ladies. Fans fluttered, feathered headdresses bobbed, and voices squealed. She gritted her teeth. She really did not like large, giddy gatherings. Through the imposing doors at the side of the ballroom, she could see the hall that led to the ladies' retiring room. Escape beckoned. Lynley would have to hunt spies on his own.

Before she could take a step, her arm was seized in a painful grip, and she was yanked from the room. In the hall her captor spun her around and pushed her to the wall. She looked up into the smooth, cool face of Lord Barksted.

"You wanted a word with me?" She looked pointedly at the man's hand on her arm. "You had only to ask."

Barksted's bold glance dropped to Emily's bosom. "Happy for you, Miss Radstock, that you landed a fiancé after so long a time on the shelf. Apparently, Lynley likes shop-worn goods."

"Happy for you, Lord Barksted, that in being so long on the town yourself, no woman need go to the trouble of liking you at all."

A look of menace passed over Barksted's face, exposing yellow, tobacco-stained teeth clenched tight. "You'll have to do better than that to insult me, miss."

He expected her to cower, but Emily drew herself up and leaned toward him, enduring the spirits on his breath. "And you'll have to grow some wit if you wish to remain a welcome guest anywhere."

From within the ballroom came the first notes of the opening quadrille. Guests hurried past them through the grand doors. Barksted glanced round and seemed to recall their surroundings.

He inhaled and spoke again. "Your fiancé is as meddlesome as he is handsome. If you wish Lynley to retain the perfection of his features, you will exercise your influence to keep him from sticking his oar in my business."

"Would that be the business of intimidating women?"

His grip tightened painfully on her arm. "I should have known that you and Lynley were a pair of meddlers."

Emily felt the danger of slapping him or planting him a facer. He was a man who would hurt a woman. She glanced across the hall at the door to the retiring room. "Lord Barksted, consider where you are and to whom you speak. Do not imagine me unprotected in the world, and do not imagine that your own credit can withstand such ill-bred behavior."

"Neither your sex nor your title protects you from my wrath should you or your imbecilic fiancé cross me again, Lady Emily."

Some commotion in the hall made Barksted turn his head. A gentleman barreled into him, loosening his hold.

"Ravenhurst," he cried, reaching for the man's arm. "Look where you're going, man."

Emily stepped sideways and dashed for the retiring room.

The room reserved for Lady Vange's female guests was lined with benches and fitted up with painted screens for privacy and tall cheval glasses for preening. Six women received the attentions of two chambermaids and a lady's dresser, assisting with repairs to dress and appearance and offering mild refreshments to those who might feel faint.

The utterly feminine scene was at odds with Emily's rage. She wanted to tear Lord Barksted limb from limb. He was a despicable man, much worthier of a firing squad than poor Chunee.

She waved off an approaching maid and headed for the privacy of one of the screens. She needed to recover her calm, and then she needed to find Lynley. As she neared the screen, she heard sobs coming from behind it. She glanced a question at the dresser, who shrugged her shoulders.

The bereft sobbing continued with great gusts, which could not be good for anyone wearing stays. Evidently, someone was having a worse time than Emily.

Emily picked up a glass of lemonade and approached.

"Hello," she said.

There was a pause in the sobs.

"I'm coming in," said Emily.

"No one must see me."

"It's only me." Emily peeked around the screen. A golden-haired young woman in the white of a girl's first Season had curled up in a chair between a side table and a standing glass. Her eyes and nose were red, and her over-elaborate coiffure tilted disastrously to one side.

She straightened, glanced at Emily, and gave a hiccup. "Do I know you?"

"Not at all, so you won't mind my help. Here, drink this."

The girl accepted the lemonade and drank. She was the sort of ripe, delicate beauty, all rosy-cheeked and dewy-eyed, usually besieged by suitors.

"Whatever has happened to overset you?" Emily asked.

The girl sniffed and fumbled for her reticule. A pair of men's tan York gloves slid from her lap to the floor. Immediately, she began to sob again, her bosom heaving, and the lemonade sloshed dangerously in the glass.

Emily retrieved the glass and scooped up the gloves, setting both on a small round table. She stepped up to the girl and put an arm around her shoulder and held her until the storm subsided.

"What terrible thing has happened?" Emily asked.

"He gave...me...gloves."

"And?"

"He glanced and smiled at me all evening. Then he strolled over and handed me gloves." She shuddered.

"Who is he?"

"Archer."

Emily glanced again at the gloves, a man's good quality tan York gloves. If Archer had brought the gloves to the Vange ball, did that mean he expected to meet the gloves' owner? "Whose gloves are they?" she asked.

"My brother's. Archer just wanted to know how to get a pair of stupid gloves to my brother. I thought..." A sob intervened. "I thought he was going to ask me to dance. I was never so humiliated."

The girl paused to listen to the music, and Emily braced herself for more sobs. "Nothing is going right. He's dancing with *her*, and nobody knows where my stupid brother is, and my Season is ruined."

Emily drew up a stool to sit by the girl. She said nothing to diminish the girl's pain. She knew a thing or two about a ruined Season, though she was at a loss to understand how a pair of gloves had caused such despair.

"How did the gloves end up with Archer?"

"Oh, they are from Lady Ravenhurst. My brother is forever leaving things in her house or carriage."

Emily held herself very still. To the girl the gloves were a sign of a beau's indifference, but if the gloves had come from Lady Ravenhurst, there could be no doubt that they were the very gloves the spy had used at the Ravenhurst party in the foiled attempt to get government papers out of the house.

"You remember the Radical Race," the girl prompted. "That's when everything started to go wrong."

Emily did remember. She had not seen the race, but she had certainly heard about the successful attempt weeks earlier to drive a huge van pulled by four horses across the frozen lake in Hyde Park. Most of fashionable London had turned out to see the thing done. It was exactly the sort of event that the serious-minded of Emily's friends had condemned, risking horses' lives for a wager.

While one part of her mind followed the girl's association with the gloves, with another she tried to puzzle out what had happened to the gloves since. Archer must not be a spy, or he would not dispose of the gloves to this girl so casually.

"Well," said Emily, "forget the gloves and the race. What you must do is go back into that ballroom with your head held high and dance the soles of your slippers off. You must make this Archer see that you don't care a fig for his folly in pursuing an older married woman."

"Do you think so?"

Emily nodded emphatically.

"What do I do about the stupid gloves?"

"I'll take them. Who is your brother, by the way?"

"Clive Walhouse."

Emily froze. The bits and pieces of observation and gossip rearranged themselves in her brain. Clive Walhouse might be the person they sought, and this girl was the beauty Beatrix hoped her brother Archer would pursue.

The girl turned a questioning gaze up to Emily. Perhaps, Emily could do Beatrix a good turn. "Let's worry less about your brother, and more about you. Your hair needs attention."

The girl jumped up, turned to the cheval glass, and gasped in horror. "I look a fright. No one will dance with me. Ever again."

Emily took her by the shoulders and turned her away from the mirror. "What's your name?"

"Allegra."

"Let one of the maids repair your coiffure. I know a gentleman, an excellent dancer, who can whirl you about the floor for everyone to see how lovely you look and how impervious you are to the slights of foolish young men."

"Really?"

"Truly."

Chapter Fifteen

*Inevitably, the husband hunter will get herself talked
about. She may be a person of calm good sense and placid
temperament, yet the fashionable world sees her as a volatile
commodity, like one of those elements in the laboratory of the
medieval alchemist, ready to be transformed by her interaction
with the human substance around her. She must never act so as
to be censured for impertinence and want of conduct. Above all
she must never let herself be singled out for enacting a farce or
a drama on the dance floor.*

—The Husband Hunter's Guide to London

From Lynley's point of view, Lord Ravenhurst was having a bad night.
His Foreign Office friends treated him like a pariah, and now his wife
danced a waltz with a much younger man. Ravenhurst drank steadily,
lurching from one drink tray to another.

Lynley was not without sympathy. Ravenhurst appeared to be a man
caught up in currents he did not understand. No one appeared glad to see
him, and as far as Lynley could see, no one approached him. If a spy hovered
near, he had not made himself known tonight. All Lynley had gained from
watching Ravenhurst's wanderings was separation from his betrothed.

Something had changed in her with the decision that she and Lynley
would be partners in spy catching. He had yet to determine what. She had
put up a boundary between them, like a prickly hedgerow enclosing a field.
Briefly, the barrier had come down in the wake of their adventure in the
prison. But she had put it firmly back in place after her round of morning

calls the day before. Lynley's ribs no longer ached with every step. He thought that if he could manage one waltz with her, he could find a way through the barrier again.

The first waltz of the evening ended in a burst of chatter and movement. Lynley positioned himself to face a pair of doors opposite, so that he could see both ends of the ballroom as well as the entrance. As dancers cleared the floor, he spotted Emily entering the room, arm in arm with a golden-haired girl in white. He started toward her when a hand gripped his arm and spun him around.

He shook off the hand and faced Ravenhurst at the edge of the crowd.

"Lynley, I demand satisfaction." Ravenhurst waved an empty glass in Lynley's face.

Lynley noted the drunken slur. The man could not mean what the word usually implied. "Satisfaction? From whom? If your glass is empty, man, apply to a footman."

"Do you deny your attentions to my wife?"

Lynley stiffened. There it was, a direct if wrong-headed challenge. Around them heads turned, talk died. "Utterly. You'll have to pardon me, Ravenhurst, I'm about to dance with my betrothed."

Ravenhurst's eyes closed and unclosed as if he could blink away some fog. He stared at Lynley. "No, that's not what you say."

"You'll have to advise me of my lines, then, old fellow. Are we rehearsing a play?" If it was a script, Lynley guessed that someone had prompted Ravenhurst to make the challenge.

Ravenhurst straightened and went at it again. "You come to London from nowhere with an insignificant title and you make up to my wife and encourage her in folly at a gaming club. Do you deny that you were there?"

At the mention of the club, Lynley knew who was behind Ravenhurst's challenge. Barksted. If he glanced around, he would find the man watching. Lynley thought of his pistols at home at Lyndale Abbey. If anyone deserved a bullet, it was Barksted, not the poor lost soul in front of him.

"I was with Woodford."

"Woodford? The man never gambles." Ravenhurst took an unsteady step forward. "You were there to expose my wife to the contempt of society."

"Let it go, Ravenhurst. You've been misinformed."

Ravenhurst shook his head. "No, you've confused my wife, made her forget her duty to her husband and her sons. I should call you out."

Lynley's throat contracted painfully. Every instinct prompted him to answer the man's insults in kind. But this was what his father must have looked like, confronting the Russian officer who was his wife's lover:

wounded, confused, and desperate, sure that the man in front of him was the author of all his grievances.

He made himself speak calmly. "But you won't."

Ravenhurst blinked at him. "I won't?"

"Go home."

"Are you calling me a coward?" Ravenhurst's voice grew shrill.

"You're a gentleman and the father of two young sons. You have a duty to the Foreign Office."

"What do you know of my Foreign Office duties? Are you the one who's taken papers from me?" Ravenhurst staggered forward and tried to take Lynley by the lapels. The glass hindered him, so that he ended up clinging to Lynley's coat with one hand. Lynley reached out to keep the man from falling.

* * * *

Emily wished for anything solid, a cobblestone, a cricket ball, rather than a pair of gloves in her hand, something she could chuck at Lord Ravenhurst's fuddled head. She could not hear what the man had said to Lynley as she and Allegra stepped up to them, but she could guess at the folly of it from the tense, expectant faces of the onlookers. Lord Ravenhurst was enacting a drama.

When he grabbed Lynley's lapel, she could not refrain from crying out.

"Lord Ravenhurst." Emily used her most quelling voice, like her old governess calling unruly charges to order in a park. Her mother would cringe to hear of it.

Ravenhurst spun her way, managing to stand only because Lynley had a grip on his shoulder.

Emily ducked and stepped between the two men. It was a bit like being caught in a children's game of falling bridges. She reached for the glass in Ravenhurst's hand.

"Could you release Lynley's lapel, Ravenhurst? I fear you are damaging his valet's work."

"You were looking for me, Lady Emily?"

Lynley disengaged Ravenhurst's hand from his lapel.

"Yes. If you could spare a moment." Emily managed a smile for Ravenhurst and turned to Lynley. "Miss Walhouse is here for the waltz you promised her."

His brows lifted, and a brief flicker of amusement flared in his dark eyes.

With a bow to his new partner, Lynley led Miss Walhouse to the floor. Emily could hear the murmur of Lynley's voice, deep and easy, as he charmed Miss Walhouse. She could see the girl's somewhat stunned expression looking up into Lynley's face.

Emily signaled a passing footman to take the empty glass from her hand. "Lord Ravenhurst, could you give me your arm? There is a question I want to ask you about Foreign Office policy on elephants."

"Elephants?" he breathed.

Emily tucked her arm in his. His breath nearly knocked her back on her heels. "Yes. Shall we take some air?"

Resolutely, she turned away from the sight of Lynley holding the golden-haired young beauty in his arms as the music started. Emily had no cause for pangs of dismay at the sight of another woman taking her place in Lynley's arms. It was not really her place. They were spy-catching partners, not lovers. Their betrothal was a ruse to deceive society. She was simply eager to tell him what she'd discovered about the gloves. Well, it could wait until she got Ravenhurst out of the way.

Chapter Sixteen

Talk may be the most important element in both courtship and marriage. Not gossip, nor conversation about philosophy or the affairs of the nation, but talk that is play, talk that is a game. It is through talk that men and women chiefly play. With the exception of the hunt and cards, men and women play few games together, and yet, play, liveliness of mind, is essential to any relationship that is to last longer than a fortnight.

—*The Husband Hunter's Guide to London*

Behind them in the grand apartments of Vange House the party continued hardly abated, though the neighborhood bells were sounding four. Lynley was glad to leave the heat and din behind and breathe cool night air as he led Emily to their waiting carriage. They'd caught no spy, and he'd been too long apart from her.

Grooms and footmen bustled about, moving the line of waiting carriages along, but the noise faded away under the last stars.

"Did Ravenhurst share his views on elephant policy?" Lynley asked as he handed her into the carriage. They were alone. There were distinct advantages to being engaged. Her father, having made his bow to Lady Vange, had left hours earlier.

"Sadly, no." She yawned. "It was necessary for his lordship to commune with a potted orange tree on the terrace. When he had emptied the contents of his stomach, I sent him home."

She sank onto the seat. Lynley settled beside her, leaning back against the cushions and stretching his legs out. A carriage was a fine and private place, though not designed for a man of his height. The door closed.

"Are you going to thank me?" she asked.

"For trapping me on the dance floor with a girl whose best friend must be her looking glass?"

"For rescuing you."

"Is that what you call it?" He rapped on the roof to signal their readiness to leave, and the carriage lurched into motion.

"Yes, I call it a rescue from whatever drama Ravenhurst was enacting in full view of Lady Vange's guests."

"He was attempting to challenge me."

"Then I regret that I had nothing to chuck at his thick head."

"Someone put him up to it," he said.

"Lord Barksted."

The instant reply banished his languor. "What makes you say that?" he asked.

"Earlier in the evening Barksted encouraged me to use my influence with you to keep you out of his business."

She spoke in that matter-of-fact way of hers, intent at the moment on adjusting her cloak around her and settling more comfortably on the seat.

"Tell me more," he said. It chilled him to think that Barksted had gone after her. Somehow even in the most fashionable ballroom in London, she managed to encounter danger.

The rustling of her garments stopped. "Really, there's nothing more to tell. Except that Barksted broke away from his chat with me to chase after Ravenhurst, which rather supports the idea that Barksted put Ravenhurst up to challenging you."

"Em." Lynley turned her to face him. She wore no bonnet. Her hair was simply parted, coiled, and secured with a row of pearls and roses. The scent of warm woman and crushed rose petals filled his head. "You have a remarkable way of not telling me what I ask."

She started to protest, but he put a finger to her lips. The carriage moved steadily through the dark streets. He lifted her onto the sloping plane of his body and settled her against him so that they pressed hip to hip.

"How are your ribs?" she asked, a little catch in her breath.

"They'll survive. Tell me everything that happened between you and Barksted."

"We have more important things to talk about."

"Do we?"

She fumbled a little, her hands under her cloak, her body twisting against his. Just that, a little movement, a brush of female parts against male parts, and his thoughts veered back to the question she'd asked him about lovemaking in a carriage. It could be done, he knew. What man hadn't thought of it? What mother hadn't warned her daughter about the perils of being alone in a closed carriage with a man?

Between them were layers of wool and silk, but under the frothy cloud of her skirts, only a thin veil of muslin covered the heat and soft, liquid center of her. He raised one of his hands to his mouth and pulled the glove off with his teeth.

Then she held up a pair of gloves between them. Even in the uncertain light of the carriage lamps, Lynley recognized those gloves. His grip tightened on her waist. "Where did you get them?"

"In the ladies' retiring room."

"Ah, a place no gentleman can enter. Feeling clever, are you?" She was clever. He liked that about her. He lifted his bare hand to push aside the curls around her ear. She shivered at the touch.

"Exactly. Archer. He gave them to Allegra Walhouse to give to her brother Clive. Apparently, neither his friend Archer nor his sister Allegra knows where Walhouse is, but he could be our man, couldn't he?"

The question was important, he knew, but he had found the edge of her skirts and worked his ungloved hand under them to take hold of one warm, muslin-covered thigh, just above the back of her knee. He pulled gently. Her knee bent, and he guided it to the bench.

"Lynley?" she stilled.

"I don't want you to slide to the floor," he said. The change made his head swim. It brought the warm cove of her body at the apex of her thighs in flush alignment with the ridge of his cockstand. A tilt of his hips would bring them both pleasure.

Then she waved the gloves in his face again with one hand, while the other hand pressed firmly against his chest. The pressure of her palm against him sent urgent messages to his cock to move against her. "Do you know where Clive Walhouse is?" she asked.

He held himself as still as he could in the moving coach and made his brain work. "Our information is that he left the country."

"*Our* information? As in you and others? You and some other partner?"

"As in the Foreign Office."

"And how do you get that information?"

"Remember, Em, there are things I can't tell you." As soon as he spoke, she tensed in his hold.

"Lynley, we're almost home. You can let me go now."

His body protested. He was enjoying her weight against him. She seemed unaware of the nature of the contact, or the thinness of the barriers of silk and wool and linen and propriety between them. Her breath reached him, smelling of sugar and oranges. She had let down her guard, not through a waltz as Lynley had planned, but through talk about the case. There was a lesson there, his brain said. *Pay attention.* His body, meanwhile, said, *Kiss her.*

He tried a compromise. "You did good spy work tonight, Em."

"What's next, do you think?"

"This," he said, and he kissed her. And realized that he had been wanting to do so for some time. In the carriage after the opera when she'd pushed him away, on the sofa in the drawing room when she'd discovered that he was a spy, in the carriage after their escape from the prison when he had wanted to strip off her black gown, and now, and in between, whenever he'd thought of her. He didn't know what she would say next, but her mouth intrigued him.

He had only a moment. In the back of his brain, he knew the coachman was bringing the horses to a stop. The footman, however weary he might be, would jump down to open the door.

But under his mouth hers softened and opened. She kissed with ardor and inexperience, and something more elusive, something he hadn't felt before.

He was trying to name that rare element in her kiss and at the same time thinking there were still too many garments between them, when she broke away from the kiss and pushed against his chest. He let her slide off of him and kept her from falling.

The carriage stopped, rocking and settling into stillness, while Lynley's body throbbed in protest. His blood raced on in his veins.

He had always had contempt for his uncle's weakness in the face of temptation. His uncle had been a man whose eye followed every exposed bosom, whose hands had reached to grab every swaying hip that passed. Lynley had believed himself immune to the temptations of coarse abundance. He had not realized that something else, something very different, something one could not squeeze and hold and press oneself against, could yet provoke strong desire, something made of wit and sharpness and fierce independence.

Beside him on the bench she righted herself in a furious rustle of garments. He reminded himself that neither of them wanted marriage. Their engagement was a cover. He might enjoy the temptation, but he must not give in to it. The door opened, and he climbed down to help her alight. Instead of taking his hand, she slapped the pair of gloves into it and descended without his assistance.

"I assume you'll want to begin looking for Clive Walhouse as soon as possible."

"Tomorrow."

"You mean today." She lifted one dark brow. "I do have one piece of further information for you."

Chapter Seventeen

The husband hunter must be under no illusion that the path to happiness is perfectly straight and smooth, for it is a shifting path made of the smallest grains of human experience—our feelings. Varied, changeable, and passing in rapid succession, they are the most difficult to fix in our minds. Who among us remembers at the end of a carriage ride precisely how we were rattled, shaken, and jolted along the way? Both the husband hunter and the gentleman who appears interested in her may mistake or misread their feelings through inattention or distraction. A dangerous moment arises in the growth of a sincere attachment, when one or the other first realizes the true nature of his or her feelings with no certainty that those feelings are returned.

—The Husband Hunter's Guide to London

Lynley tossed the pair of York gloves onto Goldsworthy's desk. He'd slept until one, and now late afternoon light streaked through the room's shutters, making a slanting pattern across the floor. The big desk stood in the shadows at the back of the room, its surface illuminated by a single lamp. Goldsworthy looked up from the usual pile of scattered papers.

"Do we have concrete evidence that Walhouse left the country?" Lynley asked.

Goldsworthy took up the gloves. "Strong signs, lad. He took his passport and emptied his bank account. No one has seen him in weeks."

"Those gloves suggest a different story." Lynley sat opposite the big man.

Goldsworthy raised one brow. "What story?"

"It turns out Archer was supposed to give the gloves to Walhouse."

"Are you sure?"

Lynley nodded and explained that Archer had given the gloves to Allegra Walhouse to give to her brother. He omitted Emily's role in acquiring the gloves.

Goldsworthy regarded him from under craggy russet brows. "And Miss Walhouse gave you the gloves?"

"I danced with her at Lady Vange's party last night. Whoever wrote the note we intercepted thinks Walhouse is within reach and interested in government documents." Lynley kept his face expressionless, aware of Goldsworthy's scrutiny and the big man's capacity for seeing through the holes in a story.

"That's a new slant on things, lad," Goldsworthy said. His eyes shifted back and forth in thought.

"What's the old slant?" Lynley asked.

Goldsworthy frowned. "We suspect that when Walhouse worked as Chartwell's secretary, he leaked information about the mission of an agent named George Fawkener to Malikov. Walhouse had a motive. His family was deep in debt, and his father was Fawkener's nearest male relative. If Fawkener stayed missing or dead, Walhouse's father, Lord Strayde, would inherit the estate."

"So Walhouse gained personally from stealing papers about Fawkener. What's the connection to Ravenhurst?"

Goldsworthy shook his head. "Malikov is the connection there. He was a frequent guest at the house. He was with Ravenhurst in the park during the Radical Race when there was an attempt on Jane Fawkener's life."

"When did the Ravenhurst papers go missing?"

"Sadly, that's where the link breaks down. The papers disappeared shortly *after* Malikov's arrest. The Russian was in a cell, and Walhouse had fled. George Fawkener himself searched Walhouse's room and found no Foreign Office material."

"Someone else must have known about the Ravenhurst papers."

Goldsworthy let out a snort of disgust. "Ravenhurst has a damned loose tongue. Half of fashionable London knows he prides himself on the contents of his red box."

He tossed the gloves back at Lynley.

"You think the gloves are a dead end?" Lynley thought of the message he'd found in those gloves—*I depend on you*—a message he now knew was intended for Walhouse. He couldn't make sense of it. Who needed to depend on a man cut off from family and friends, in hiding from the authorities?

Goldsworthy waved one of his huge hands. "No, lad. If you want another go at Walhouse, have at it, but try not to tip off the family or the servants. We'd still like to catch the fellow. You can use Wilde to get you into the house if you need to search the room again. He's got ties to the cook."

Goldsworthy returned to the study of his papers, and Lynley went in search of Wilde.

* * * *

"Lynley, explain the plan to me again." Emily had lost the argument about what role she was to play in the search of Clive Walhouse's room. Another day of spying, and once again she was to be the "distractor." She had agreed because it made sense, and because he had been willing to tell her something more of the case. But she drew a line at what she was willing to do.

"If you think I'm going to knock over the tea table in Lady Strayde's drawing room, or throw china, think again."

Their carriage pulled up at some distance from the Walhouse townhouse. Teddy Walhouse, Lord Strayde, continued to occupy the house that belonged to his cousin George Fawkener, even though Fawkener had returned alive from a mission abroad. Apparently, George Fawkener was both indifferent to the property and generous to his family.

"Could you faint?" Lynley asked.

"You know me better than that." She laughed.

"You'll think of something. And remember—"

"I'm not to mention the missing brother. I know."

He leaped down, shut the door, and signaled the coachman to drive on.

It was a bright April day. The street bustled with activity. The neighborhood bells rang one, the perfect hour for a morning call. No moonlight. No kiss, no backward glance, just partners moving forward to trap a spy. It was as if the kiss in the carriage had never happened. She did not understand how he could be so wholly unaffected while his kiss had kept her awake for hours, her body bubbling with energy like a spring-fed brook.

The plan was for Lynley to meet a confederate of his in the guise of a former servant known to the staff in the kitchen. Emily meanwhile was to pay a call and create enough distraction for Lynley's confederate to sneak Lynley up to Clive Walhouse's room for a search. She had no idea what he hoped to find. Like her, Lynley would be making up the plan as he went along.

He liked that. He liked uncertainty and risk, and she had to admit that she did, too. That was why the kiss in the carriage had stayed with her. She had liked it because it had been risky, like going in disguise to see Malikov, not because her heart was softening toward Lynley. She had to be clear about these matters.

Once again, she noted the calling cards on a silver dish as she handed her hat and gloves to a footman. She followed him up one branch of a forked staircase under the eye of Admiral Nelson's famous spyglass pointing down at her from a magnificent painting on the wall.

In the drawing room, the butler announced her to Lady Strayde and Allegra, sitting on a black and gold striped sofa chatting with another lady and her two daughters. The girls had their backs straight, hands folded primly in laps, bosoms proudly lifted.

Emily strode forward. The three girls, younger than Roz, stared. Emily wondered whether she should have brought a cane or a Bath chair, or worn an old maid's cap, but she had forgotten about the ring, Lynley's ring. It was the ring to which every female eye in the room immediately turned. She took the offered seat, keeping the ring in view, as the first pleasantries were exchanged.

Emily recognized the scene as one she'd endured in her first Season, the girls obliged to sit demurely silent while their mothers exchanged competing narratives of their daughters' triumphs in society.

"And then Mr. Talbot danced the second waltz with Marianne," Lady Rivers was saying. "We thought perhaps we'd see your son there, Lady Strayde."

Allegra gave her mother a quick pleading glance at the mention of Clive, but Lady Strayde was made of sterner stuff and simply said, "I'm sorry you missed him."

Emily took a sip of the tea she'd been offered, looking about for some means of distraction that would bring the servants running. The tea tray sat securely on a low table. A pretty fire screen was in place, so she could hardly faint from the heat. Then she caught the younger of Lady Rivers's daughters staring at the ring.

"You must wonder," she said, "at my betrothed's choice of ring."

Lady Rivers gently pressed her daughter Marianne's chin up, closing the girl's astonished mouth.

"He brought it from Spain, and of course, it's the history of the thing that made him think of it for me. But enough of my ring. I came to see how you were, Miss Walhouse, and whether you enjoyed Lady Vange's ball."

At the mention of the Vange ball it was Lady Rivers's turn to stiffen. Emily's remark had given a point to Lady Strayde. Allegra seized the conversational opening, pleased to name the partners she'd enjoyed after her dance with Lynley. Lady Rivers retaliated with a catalogue of morning callers and posies received by her two girls.

Emily looked about again. Really, she could not prolong the visit any further without straining the bonds of politeness. An extraordinarily ugly vase on the mantel caught her eye. She set her cup aside and considered whether the vase would break if it slipped from her hands to the carpet, or whether she might have to drop the thing on the tea table.

Just when she thought it must be the table, the door to the drawing room opened, and a large gray puppy with a black muzzle burst into the room and bounded toward Allegra, who jumped to her feet shrieking, "No, not my gown!"

A younger girl burst into the room after the dog. She called, "Come, Ulysses" to no avail.

Emily snatched a macaroon from the tea tray and called the dog. He heard his name, paused to look at her outstretched hand, and hurled himself her way. Emily stepped squarely in his path and let herself be knocked backward and down. The puppy pinned her skirts to the floor with wet, muddy paws, belatedly remembering his manners and coming to a sit. Emily tossed the macaroon in the direction of the tea table, and the puppy scrambled after it, circling the table madly, bumping against the corners, setting cups and saucers rattling, and leaving a muddy trail across the pale Aubusson carpet.

Lady Rivers's daughters squealed and pulled their skirts close. Allegra wailed that the dog ruined everything. Lady Strayde signaled the girl at the door to pull the bell. Servants came running. Emily pulled herself to her feet and surveyed her ruined gown. She hoped Lynley knew what to do with his opportunity.

* * * *

At the tradesman's entrance Lynley checked his watch, which assured him that more than twenty minutes had elapsed since Emily's morning call had begun. He wondered if she'd lost her nerve. Then Wilde stuck his head out the door. "Quick," he said with a grin. "The dog's got into the drawing room. Ten minutes."

Lynley followed Wilde through the kitchen to the servants' stairs, scrambled up three flights to the bedroom floor, and slipped into the room that belonged to the absent Clive Walhouse. Closed drapery made the room dark and cool. The walls were pale gold above dark wood paneling, the hangings and drapery a deep green. The room smelled of dead coal fires, leather, and scent—a faintly familiar woman's scent. It stopped Lynley just inside the door. He turned from the hearth and let his gaze sweep the room, passing over the mahogany desk with its large surface and three shallow drawers across the front. It had been searched. He had seen a list of the contents of the desk in a report: paper, pens, and pen-mending implements, an engagement calendar, and boxes of calling cards in neat order, a drawer filled with cards of invitation and another with unpaid bills from tradesmen.

He moved a few steps away from the hearth, trying to locate the source of the scent. There was a heavy opulence to the room, but few signs of Walhouse's presence. A pair of silver trays, one on each bedside table, displayed combs and brushes and scent bottles.

Lynley lifted a lid and smelled the man's pomade. It was not the scent that had teased his senses when he entered. It occurred to him that Walhouse would not be obvious. He had carried on as a spy under Chartwell's nose, so he must have learned means of concealment.

Lynley went back to the door and waited for the elusive scent to reach him again. The room was too ordinary, too neat, too lacking in anything distinctive except for the few articles on the trays that suggested Walhouse's vanity. Lynley could feel it. Walhouse expected to escape detection by appearing ordinary.

Lynley let his gaze wander again, looking for an object that was out of place, unexpected. Nothing caught his notice. He closed his eyes to concentrate on the scent. It was near and to his right. When he opened his eyes again, he noticed the umbrella stand next to the door, dark wood with a brass interior. A half dozen walking sticks and an umbrella stood there. The stand was quiet, unobtrusive, serviceable, meant to be overlooked.

Lynley leaned closer and caught the cloying floral scent. He grabbed the sticks and lifted them out of the stand. The black umbrella bulged oddly. He opened it and found a packet of papers bound to the shaft with black ribbon. Lynley untied the ribbon and grabbed hold of the packet. A sharp rap sounded on the door. He shoved the papers into his waistcoat. Wilde's voice came from the hall. "Sir, time to go."

As they came down the stairs, Lynley could hear a commotion in the kitchen, and Wilde indicated another passage. Lynley followed and they emerged under the stairs in the front entry. Above them someone was descending.

Lynley crossed the foyer to the door, turning to face whoever it was, as if he had just arrived. He looked up into a painted scene of battle with Lord Nelson peering down through his famous spyglass.

Then Emily appeared, her head high, her eyes dancing with mirth, her blue gown torn and streaked with mud. The butler and a footman followed after her.

"Oh, hello, Lynley." She waved from above. "I hope I didn't keep you waiting." She came down the last flight.

"I've only just arrived," he said, offering his arm.

While the butler hovered anxiously, Emily accepted her gloves and bonnet from the footman.

Lynley had hardly noticed her gown before, but now he saw how perfectly the blue gown's simplicity suited her and how ruined it was. He handed her into the carriage and climbed in after her. "What happened to you? Apparently, you did not find any glassware to drop."

She grinned at him. "I was luckier this time. There was an unexpected entrance of a mastiff pup in the drawing room. More to the point, did you find anything?"

"This," he said. He undid the top buttons of his waistcoat and pulled out the bundle.

"What is it?" she asked. She lifted it to her nose and gave him a questioning glance. "Scented paper?"

"Do you recognize the scent?" he asked.

She sniffed again, and shook her head. "A woman's perfume." He obviously recognized it.

"Shall we get you home and out of your ruined gown?"

She shot him a quick, searching glance. "Oh no. You're not leaving me behind while you go off with those papers. Open them."

Chapter Eighteen

It may be that a particular gentleman comes straight to the husband hunter's side directly he enters a room. With him she falls into easy conversation. A tacit understanding exists between the husband hunter and this gentleman that reserves to him the last set of the evening. No declaration has been made, and yet he will confide in her as to the size of the park at his estate, and the sad state of the drawing room furnishings there since his dear mama's death. In such a case, the husband hunter may be pardoned for assuming the conquest of his heart complete. But she must pause, for she and her charming beau are as yet untested in love.

—*The Husband Hunter's Guide to London*

Lynley gave her an approving look as Emily drew off her gloves.

"What do we have?" she asked. He removed the packet from his waistcoat. An unexpected puff of breeze ruffled the scraps of paper in his hand, and he pinned them against his thigh. Emily slipped the top scrap from the pile. "What is it?"

"A note of hand, an IOU."

"Not missing government papers?"

He shook his head. "But hidden. Walhouse did not want these papers discovered."

Emily collected the little notes, carefully shuffling through them. Each had a sum, a date, and Lady Ravenhurst's name. The largest sum, fifty guineas, made Emily gasp. Over the winter Lady Ravenhurst had played deep and lost badly at least eight times. A gentleman was obliged to pay his debts of honor promptly and without complaint. A woman, a wife at any rate, unless she had control of her money, would have to apply to her husband to pay such sums as Lady Ravenhurst owed.

She looked up at Lynley. "Is this what she and Ravenhurst argued about the night of the party? Does she owe Clive Walhouse this much? It's staggering."

The breeze had begun to rise, making them huddle together on the curricle's bench, sheltering the papers.

"Take them," he said. She tucked them in her reticule. He unfolded the larger pages that formed the packet and spread them on his leg.

"What is this one?" she asked.

They leaned together, shoulder to shoulder to read the thing. "It's a lease in Walhouse's name on a terrace house off the Marylebone Road."

Even with the legal terms of the document, Emily could see that Walhouse had leased it for the Season. "Could he be living there, hiding in the midst of London?"

Lynley shook his head, frowning.

Emily could see that he was thinking, putting information together in his head. "You haven't told me, by the way, what you know of his disappearance."

"You think I know something?" he asked.

She raised a brow. "Of course you do."

He laughed and told her briefly about Walhouse's connection to Malikov and the Foreign Office and the problem of the timing for his involvement in the loss of the Ravenhurst papers.

"So he was gone or in hiding before the Ravenhurst papers disappeared," she said. "But his sister says he was forever leaving things with Lady Ravenhurst, gloves, hat, cloak. So he clearly had a connection with the lady. What troubles you?"

His mouth was a grim line. "It's not a hiding place. Look where it is. Think of the terms of the lease."

Emily turned back to the document. She read again the description of the furnished rooms, the starting and ending dates of the lease, the discreet address. She was conscious of Lynley, like a tutor, waiting for a slow pupil to understand some obvious concept.

"Oh," she said, "it's the sort of house a man takes for his mistress." As soon as she said it, she turned to him. "Lady Ravenhurst and Clive? What about the IOUs? Could they be...lovers if she owed him so much money?"

"I don't know. It's possible. When Ravenhurst challenged me, he accused me of exposing his wife to embarrassment in that gaming hell."

"You think it may have been Clive Walhouse?" Emily had a reticule full of notes that suggested just that.

Lynley didn't answer right away. "You know there's an uglier possibility here."

"What?"

Lynley looked out over the horses' heads. The chill wind was growing stronger, blowing the animals' manes and rattling their harness. "It's possible that Walhouse paid her debts in exchange for..."

"Her favors." Emily completed the thought. She remembered Lady Ravenhurst's profound unhappiness the night of the party, her inability to congratulate Emily on her engagement. She took a deep breath. "We're speculating, aren't we? We don't know the truth. We should not jump to ungenerous interpretations without more evidence."

His face remained hard and closed. He had withdrawn into himself to some memory or association. From their first night together, Lady Ravenhurst had been a figure in the background of every scene, and Emily was no nearer to understanding what the lady meant to Lynley than she had been that first evening.

Emily thought of all she'd seen and heard. Most likely Archer's wager had been about Lady Ravenhurst and Walhouse, but perhaps he had got it wrong. The wager had been that an unhappy wife would take a lover. It was the way of the fashionable world. A woman constrained to marry a man of her family's choosing could take a lover once she had produced the required heir. Lady Ravenhurst might be pleasing herself through an affair with Clive Walhouse, or she might be caught up in something not of her choosing.

The wind had become brisk and cold. Clouds of tarnished silver piled up above them, darkening the day. The mud had hardly dried on Emily's skirts. She would ask her maid to brush them later, though she was not sure the gown could be saved. But it was a gown after all, not a marriage. "In any case, Lady Ravenhurst's unhappiness, her gaming debts, those are not our concern. We're after missing government papers." As she said it, she looked up and met his gaze.

"Willing to risk a soaking?" he asked.

She glanced at the heavy sky. They weren't going far, just beyond the Marylebone Road. Her bonnet and cloak had no great pretensions to fashion. She nodded. "Is your groom willing?"

Lynley looked back at the young man.

"Then we investigate the house," he said. His grin returned, and she felt once more that she understood him. There was a risk to be taken, and he was happy to take it. She looked down again at her ruined skirts, to hide how pleased she felt at that *we*.

* * * *

The sky, which had been so bright and sunny at one, was nearly black when they reached the quiet, out-of-the-way street named in the lease. The buildings were new, part of the grand architectural schemes of the king when he had been regent. The park named in his honor was supposed to open to the public one day. The crescent where Clive Walhouse had rented a place was three stories of white stone. Each small but elegant apartment had a tall, narrow entry that jutted out from the building, iron railings around the ground floor and a balcony off the first-story window.

"How are we to get in?" she asked Lynley as they approached.

He glanced up and down the street. A few pedestrians hurried past as the sky blackened and the wind shook the trees. He escorted her to the little covered entry and told her to wait while he found a way in through the back. She stood under the roof, out of sight as he drove off.

Between the heavy dark clouds and the ground, the sky took on a violet hue. The air waited, charged and squeezed between cloud and earth. A closed carriage passed slowly down the street, the driver on the box turning to stare at the house, and Emily shrank further into the shadow of the little roof.

Finding missing papers was the sort of game she and Frederick and Roz had often devised for a summer's afternoon at Candover. Mother would take some treasure from the attics to hide in a hollow tree trunk or a crumbling stone wall, and they would follow the clues she set until darkness or rain sent them back inside for cakes and lemonade. But the papers for which she and Lynley searched mattered to some clever, ruthless enemy who would kill to possess them.

Abruptly, lightning flashed and vanished. The street disappeared in blackness. Emily held her breath. The world returned, thunder boomed, and rain fell in a straight gush.

Behind Emily the door opened. Relieved, she turned and started forward, recoiling as she met not Lynley, but a stranger in a rough coat with a round-crowned felt hat pulled low over his bearded face.

"Hah," he said, grinning at her. "I know you."

Emily shook her head. "You most certainly do not." She backed out of the little porch. The rain hit her, and plastered her bonnet and cloak to her person. She whirled and dashed for the street, but the closed carriage she'd seen earlier pulled up at the end of the walkway, trapping her between the iron railings and the stranger. He grabbed her cloak and yanked hard. She staggered and reached for the iron railing. Her captor put his arms around her waist, trying to shake her loose. Her bonnet fell forward, obscuring her vision. Rain pelted her, soaking her gloves and sending cold trickles down her nape. Her captor smelled rank and sour. He heaved her up off her feet, and she lost her hold on the slick iron.

"Look what I found, Dicky," he called to the carriage driver. "Wager we'll be well paid to give 'er back to 'er husband," he said, wrestling her toward the carriage.

Emily clawed at the arms around her waist and tried to plant her feet. "Let me go." Her skirts clung to her legs.

"Ye need to learn not to run off..." The words ended in a high-pitched yelp. Emily was free, and the man was down on his side on the flagstones, curled in a ball, Lynley standing over him.

The driver of the carriage shouted something that was lost in another crash of thunder.

Lynley grabbed her hand and hauled her after him down the walk and into the house. He shut and bolted the door and pulled her into his arms.

"I'm so-so-so—" she started to protest, then the shivering took over. She thought she would come apart with the shaking, but Lynley held her. Their breath sounded ragged in her ears.

They stood dripping on the entry stones. Beyond them a narrow, carpeted hall extended through the gloom the length of the building. The flickering light of the storm entered from a stairwell at the midpoint of the hall. Thunder rumbled and crashed above them.

Lynley removed her bonnet and tossed it aside. He tucked her hands inside his coat against his ribs. She wanted to thank him, but could not keep her teeth from chattering.

"You know," he said amiably, "we have to get you out of these ruined clothes."

She had to agree. She was wearing a gown of ice.

"Wait here," he said. "They won't be back. They did what they came to do before we arrived. I must have scared that fellow your way."

He pulled free, and she let him go. The cold in the house was deep. She supposed that no fire had been lit for weeks. She heard him moving in the next room. She needed to tell him the ruffian's mistake about her identity.

He returned with a lit candle. "Upstairs," he said. "Let's get you warm."
They climbed by the candle's steady glow and the storm's sudden flashes.
At the top of the stairs a hall led to a bedroom at the rear of the house.

Lynley set the candle on a dressing table, revealing a scene of disarray.
Someone had swept everything from the table to the floor, including a box
of loose powder. A streak of it lay white on the blue carpet, giving off the
powerful flowery scent of the papers Lynley had found in Clive Walhouse's
room. Dresser drawers had been emptied onto the floor, and the doors
of a tall wardrobe hung open, with a lavender silk wrapper spilling out.

Lynley ignored the mess. Standing in front of her, he stripped off her
sopping cloak. Then he took hold of her shoulders and turned her around
to fumble with the tiny buttons at the back of her gown.

"I suppose these are the height of fashion," he said. "A sensible woman
would have buttons a man could see."

Emily thought a sensible woman would not be mixed up with wardrobe-
wrecking spies and ruffians.

With the same brisk efficiency with which he'd removed her cloak, he
pushed the gown over her shoulders and down past her hips. He untied
the tapes at her waist to let her petticoat fall around her ankles. She felt
him hesitate, his hands still at her waist, then he began to undo the laces
of her stays. Her corset dropped to the floor.

Taking her hand, he turned her toward him and helped her step out of
the pile of wet garments. Then he stopped moving. In the gap between
intention and action, he simply gazed at her.

The candle's glow enclosed them in a circle of wan golden light.

Her skin burned with the cold. Her hair dripped. Stinging rivulets of
water trickled down her back and shoulders. Her ordinary, white lawn
undergarments clung to her skin like sticking plasters.

A man of sense would see a melting figure of ice, like some frozen
sculpture dissolving amid the fruits and desserts at the end of a grand party.
Lynley stood transfixed. Emily had never seen the look on his face before.

She shivered, and he recovered and turned to the bed. He tore apart the
coverings, pulling out a quilt and wrapping her in a cocoon of warmth. His
hands moved over the quilt in a steady chafing motion. Emily let him warm
her, keeping her jaw clamped shut, waiting for the violent chills to stop.

"That fellow must have searched the house," he said. "I recognized him,
one of Barksted's hirelings."

She wanted to tell him what the man had said, but she could not keep
her teeth from chattering.

He kissed her mouth briefly, his lips warm and firm. "Tell me later," he said. He pressed her head to his chest and kept up the chafing motion.

The storm drummed on the roof and water ran in sheets down the windows. The flicker of lightning and rumble of thunder moved north. When the chills subsided, she tried to speak again.

"Better?" he asked. She nodded against his chest. "Wait here. I'll get a fire going."

He stepped away, and Emily stared at the bed. The frame was heavy, dark wood. From the tall posts hung gorgeous blue and white bed curtains. Lynley's attack on the covers revealed layers of sacking and straw stuffing piled under a mattress, pillows, and silken coverlet. It was a bed in which the princess would never feel the pea. When the bed curtains were pulled, the sleepers would be in a private world. It struck Emily that the house existed solely to hold this bed from which the rest of the world could be shut out. Outside, storms could rage. Inside it, the lovers would only be aware of each other.

Lynley returned with another candle, a bottle of wine, and two glasses. He lit the coals in the hearth and made them a nest of bedding and pillows on the floor. He settled Emily against the pillows, poured the wine, and stretched out beside her.

"Help is on the way," he said.

"Help?" She managed to hold the glass he offered without spilling.

"I've sent for two reliable people. They'll come with a closed carriage, and some things we need to get you safely home."

She should be relieved, but she felt flat instead. She'd ended up soaked and useless. Their adventure would end before it began, without finding the spy. They had two mysteries to solve, and the questions remained unanswered. What trouble had Lady Ravenhurst gotten herself into and what had happened to her husband's papers?

"This house is a lovers' hideaway, isn't it?" she asked Lynley. "What were Barksted's men looking for, do you think?"

"Something to give Barksted a hold over Lady Ravenhurst. He knows she has a gaming habit, but apparently Walhouse held her IOUs, the ones we found."

"Did Walhouse buy her then?" Emily shivered again, recalling Lady Ravenhurst's bleak look of despair the night of her party.

Lynley nodded. "And Barksted wants to be the next man to have a hold over her, but his bully boys did us a favor with their search."

"They did?"

He set his glass aside and withdrew a piece of paper from his coat pocket.

"What is it?" she asked.

"A letter," he said. "A complaint from a neighbor of Clive Walhouse's father in Kent."

"That's an odd thing to find here, isn't it?" she asked.

"Very," he said. "Read it."

Emily, too, put down her glass, and leaned against him, their shoulders touching. The writer charged that Lord Strayde was negligent in his duty of appointing a new curate to the living in the neighborhood of Longfield. The people were suffering for lack of attentions of a clergyman, and he urged Lord Strayde to delay no longer, but to do his duty. The letter was recent.

She sat up. "It puts Walhouse here, doesn't it? Immediately before his disappearance?"

"Yes."

"Oh," she said. "You think he's gone to this empty parsonage. It's not too far from London, and it's on the Dover road."

"Stop," he said, taking the letter from her hands and stuffing it back in his coat.

"Stop what?" she asked.

"Thinking, figuring things out."

"Why?"

"Because," he said, pushing her down into the pile of bedding and rolling to pin her there with his body. "It makes me want to do this." He lay above her, propped on his elbows, looking down into her face. His hands touched her hair. His heavy-lidded gaze met hers, his dark eyes full of longing.

He was going to kiss her. It made no sense. One moment they were speaking of the mystery, and the next his body was pressed to hers.

She must look like a drowned cat fished from the river and wrapped in cotton batting. But in his eyes she saw herself, not as the spinster society mocked and her family despaired of, the spinster she protected from the world's scorn with her important work. In his eyes she was another Emily, desirable, passionate, alive.

Her lips parted, thoughts of spies and papers fled, and her whole self stilled to receive that kiss.

And then it came. He leaned down. His imperfect mouth met hers, and heat shot through her, warming her everywhere at once. Emily arched up into his kiss, returning heat for heat. He smelled of rain-dampened wool and himself, a heady mixture of wood and spice and man that Emily would know anywhere.

She reached up, circling his back with her arms, containing him in the world of her arms, relishing the pressure of his chest against her breasts. He wore entirely too many clothes.

The kiss deepened, and she opened her mouth. His tongue met hers in a frankly carnal exchange, an invitation to throw off all restraint. A new and unexpected sensation spread through her limbs, burning away doubt and hesitation. With Lynley she realized, she could be freely and unabashedly herself, however flawed, muddied and disheveled, or obstinate and headstrong. She could even be that thing ladies were never permitted to be—clever. She kissed him back with open longing.

Through the layers of clothing and quilt he pressed urgently against her, as if his whole self strained to join her whole self. With one hand he tugged at the quilt, pulling it aside.

He lifted his face from hers and gazed down a little dazedly at her breasts.

"Now," he said, his voice low and rough, "would be a good time to say no, if you wish it. There will be no gossip. Barksted's men don't know who you are."

Cool air puckered the tips of her breasts. He had offered her a moment to regain control, as he had that day in the park when he'd seized Circe's reins. Emily had only to pull the quilt around her. She knew the rules of her world, knew the limits of their partnership. She wore the heavy, lavish ring he'd bestowed on her, itself a sign that their betrothal was a show, an illusion, like a scene from the opera. *But*, whispered a voice she could not still, *you want this.*

"Yes," she said.

A brief joy flashed in his dark eyes before his lids descended, his gaze fastened on her breasts. His left hand circled her right breast lightly through the thin lawn of her chemise. Then he lowered his mouth and took full possession, his teeth and lips drawing sensation from the taut nipple, sending pleasure streaking deep through her to gather and pool in the intimate place between her legs. She reached under his waistcoat and tugged at his shirttails, eager to put her hands to his flesh.

Her mind was empty of words. Sensation overwhelmed her.

Again he joined their mouths. He made a low noise in his throat, and his knee nudged her legs apart. She stilled, alert to the change, a lifetime's habits of propriety in the sudden stiffness of her knees.

Abruptly, she felt him pull back.

Chapter Nineteen

The husband hunter must not rely on the honor of a gentleman with whom she has formed the merest acquaintance at a ball or private party. She must assume that the better part of any gentleman's character will remain unknown to her until revealed in a moment that requires integrity and courage.

—*The Husband Hunter's Guide to London*

Footsteps on the stairs and voices in the hall intruded. Lynley pushed himself off Emily and rolled away, springing up to stand at the mantel looking down into the fire. Emily had only a few seconds to pull herself upright and pull the quilt around her. A sharp rap sounded, and the bedroom door opened. Help had arrived.

A pair of young persons entered the room and greeted Lynley.

"Came as quick as we could, sir," the young man said in a posh accent at odds with his appearance. He had extraordinary white teeth and ears that stuck out from an otherwise handsome young face. Next to him a girl of striking chestnut beauty bobbed a curtsy.

"Thanks, Wilde," said Lynley. Lynley appeared his cool and distant self, while every part of Emily pulsed with heat. Her heartbeat galloped, sending her blood rushing through her veins. Lynley made the introductions and took the young man off with him to finish a search of the house.

Emily and the girl, Miranda, looked at each other.

"Now that they've gone, miss," said Miranda, "let's get you warm and dry. I've brought some things for you to wear."

As good as her word, the girl laid the things she carried on the big bed. She helped Emily move near the fire, peeled away the quilt, and made quick work of helping Emily out of her still-damp undergarments. Emily found herself briefly naked, her breasts puckered, her flesh marked by lines where stays and ties had stiffened around her. Lynley's scorching kisses had left no marks.

Miranda swiftly wrapped her in a towel, keeping up a bit of chatter about the storm. Then she helped Emily into dry pantaloons, shift, and corset, and a plain gown of pale green silk. She draped a cream wool shawl over Emily's shoulders and led her to the dressing table bench.

Emily glanced once at her reflection in the glass and shuddered. It was far worse than she'd thought. The girl began to pull the pins from Emily's drooping hair.

"Are you in Lynley's employ?" Emily hardly knew how to ask the question. The girl was a competent dresser, but not like a servant.

"Oh no, miss. My father has a shop on Bond Street." She said it with a touch of pride. "Kirby's. Do you know it?"

"The chemist's?" Emily had seen the shop but had made no purchases there. The sodden mass of her hair hung down, and cold tendrils along her neck sent a quick shiver through her.

"Yes, miss."

"So, how do you know Lynley then?"

The girl picked up a brush and began to pull it through Emily's tangles. "Through Nate Wilde, of course. He's my intended. He works...with Sir Ajax."

"He's a spy then, is he?" Emily could not hide her surprise. It was odd to hear Lynley called by his proper title. She had been thinking of him as Lynley for so long.

A look almost comical in its guilt crossed Miranda's face. "Don't tell them I said anything, please." It was an earnest plea.

"Of course not." Emily waited. The girl was talkative by nature.

"Well, we help on cases sometimes. That's how we met Sir Ajax."

"Cases?"

"Mysteries that the spies must solve."

"And you two helped Lynley?"

"We were on a case for Lord Mountjoy when Sir Ajax held up the stagecoach and the guard shot Nate."

"Wait. I don't understand. You say Lynley held up a stage?" Something his aunt Silsden said came back to her.

"Oh yes, miss. He makes a fine highwayman on that big black of horse of his, and he's ever so cool with a pistol. No telling what would've become of us, if he hadn't abducted us right there and then."

"Abducted you?" It was plain that Lynley had had far more interesting adventures before he'd ever met Emily. Again Emily's spirits sank. "So who gives out these cases?"

Miranda opened and closed her mouth. "Oh, miss, sorry. I've said too much already. You won't tell them I told you anything."

"Of course not."

"Look, miss," Miranda invited, gesturing toward the mirror. "No one will ever suspect you've been having adventures."

Emily looked in the glass. It was true. She was restored to her usual appearance of sense and propriety. No one would guess that she had come so close to being seduced by a spy. She would return to her father's house looking as if she'd spent the afternoon sipping tea. Tomorrow she and Lynley would appear side by side at Roz's dinner, the picture of a properly betrothed couple.

* * * *

With her morning chocolate Emily woke to mortification. She leaned against her pillows, unable even to lift her cup. She, who prided herself on her power to direct her life's course, to act according to sense and principle, had, in a giddy moment of strong feeling, seen the promise of happiness in Lynley's dark eyes, and said yes to ruin.

Intent on the puzzle of the missing papers, she had not realized how far she'd been led down the path of seduction. For a moment it had seemed as if everything had changed between them, as if each existed only for the other. Only the fortuitous arrival of Lynley's friends had saved her. On her own, she had forgotten the precise nature and boundaries of their partnership. She had a strong inclination to pull the coverlet over her head and curl into a ball.

Next to her cooling chocolate on the tray was a note from her mother. She picked it up and read.

My dear Emily,

You may imagine that no London news reaches me at this distance, and that preoccupied as I am with Grandmama's care, I am indifferent

to the success of your Season, but make no mistake I receive regular
correspondence from a great many people.

To call Lady Vange's ball private is, I fear, to misuse the word, for a
number of persons have written in some haste to inform me that you drew
attention to yourself in the most pronounced way in the middle of the dance
floor by stepping between your betrothed and Lord Ravenhurst. As my
informants have industriously reported, you have offended every feeling
of propriety and delicacy.

I hope I am misinformed in this matter and that you will make every
use of the dinner Roz has planned to restore your credit and Lynley's in
the eyes of the fashionable world.

Ever your affectionate mother

Emily groaned, put aside the tray, and threw off the covers. At least
her mother had no idea of Emily's worst folly, and if she and Lynley could
behave with dignity at Roz's party, the gossip might fade. And she and
Lynley could return to being spy partners. This happy thought sustained
her through breakfast with only a few moments of wondering how she
would feel had they not been interrupted.

On the whole she felt she had recovered her senses when Lady Silsden
entered the drawing room in great agitation, hardly waiting for Emily's
astonished butler to announce her.

"Ma'am, you look unwell. Do sit down," Emily urged.

"You must stop him, Miss Radstock," Lady Silsden declared.

"Stop Lynley, ma'am? From what?" Emily helped her guest to a seat.

"From fighting a duel. It's all over London that he means to meet
Ravenhurst."

Emily sank onto the sofa opposite her guest. If Ravenhurst's absurd
attempt to challenge Lynley was known, then it must have been circulated
by Barksted.

"Ma'am, I'm sorry for your distress. I'm afraid you've been taken in by
some baseless tittle-tattle."

"But I hear the challenge was quite public. Everyone saw Ravenhurst
grab Lynley by his lapels at Lady Vange's ball."

There was no denying that bit. Emily could see how a clever man could
build a credible story on a drunken man's brief moment of indiscretion.
"As it happens, you're right that Ravenhurst did grab Lynley. I was there.
I can assure you that no challenge was made. Poor Lord Ravenhurst was
quite confused and in his cups."

"You don't understand. Lynley will be just like his father."

"Are you speaking of the disaster? Can you tell me what happened?"

Emily procured her guest some tea, and when Lady Silsden had recovered somewhat, Emily encouraged her to tell the story.

"It was the summer of the great victory celebrations. The Tsar was here with his sister and a great many Russian ladies and gentlemen, and officers, of course. One officer caught the eye of Lynley's mother, Caroline. The Russian was just as dashing as a soldier ought to be and quite the dancer. Lynley was with his parents in town to see all the pageantry, the reviews and enactments in the park, the fireworks at night.

"It was Lynley who realized Caroline was going to leave with the Russian. He tried to stop her as she climbed into the man's carriage, and the man whipped him. He bears the scar, you know. Then—foolish, foolish boy—he told my brother. I'm sure Lynley had no idea of what would follow. My brother should have let her go, of course, faithless jade that she was, but he pursued them, and insisted on a duel. The Russian shot him dead."

Lady Silsden held her teacup in trembling hands. Emily sat as calmly as she could. It would do no good to comment on the heartlessness of the account, but the image of Lynley's imperfect mouth intruded to stir her feelings. She knew the sequel to this story. Lynley, a boy of fourteen, had blamed himself, had believed himself at fault for failing to stop the disaster.

When Lady Silsden managed a sip of tea and put down her cup, Emily asked, "What became of his mother?"

"Oh, Caroline went off with her Russian, but he never married her. He abandoned her in Paris, I believe. She died there some years later."

"So Lynley was orphaned at fourteen?" His aunt's lack of sympathy for his lost mother could not have helped a grieving boy.

"I went to him at once. I saw that he would need the strictest guidance to avoid going down the fatal paths that had consumed his parents. I knew I would have to take him in hand. And I did."

"Then you must rely on his training and his good sense, ma'am."

"Oh, but all my work went out the window when his uncle, his mother's brother, took him away. In Spain there was nothing but debauchery." Lady Silsden frowned.

"You must have been relieved to see him when he came home from Spain looking so fit and…undissipated."

"He retreated to Lyndale, and the constables came with the tale of his being a highwayman…"

Emily gave a little start, which she hoped her guest did not notice.

"Oh, Miss Radstock, you must persuade Lynley not to fight Ravenhurst."

Lady Silsden looked like a small gray bird huddled against a storm, feathers ruffled. Emily summoned her sympathies. His aunt was an old woman, largely alone in the world, fixed in her ways, anxiously desiring her own strict idea of what was best for Lynley without any understanding of his character.

"You may rely on me to speak with him directly, ma'am. And you really must not give way to needless alarm. My sister gives her party for us tonight, as you know, ma'am, and we'll all be together."

"Of course. But if you could speak to him..."

"I shall."

"Have you set a date for your wedding?"

"We're waiting for my mother's return."

Lady Silsden nodded and looked around the room. "That's good. Perhaps your mother will have a chance to redo this room. The Egyptian mode is so out of fashion."

* * * *

Lynley left London before dawn, a pair of warring memories driving him. In one flash he would see Em in the grasp of Barksted's man, being hauled to a waiting carriage. In another flash he would see Em looking up at him, eyes alight with soft desire.

At Lyndale he found everything in its usual sober order; only Sultan was glad to see him. He wasted little time there. As he and the horse headed back to London, he wrestled his will into submission. He might want to go on spying with Emily Radstock and playing a daring game of dancing close to the flames of desire, but at the same time he knew he did not want a hired bullyboy to put rough hands on her again. She would feel betrayed that he had abandoned their partnership to act alone, but he refused to expose her to more danger, including danger from him. If they found themselves alone together again, he feared he would yield to that baser nature that his aunt had tried to check and his uncle had always encouraged.

From the moment he heard her talking to her sister Roz, he'd been intrigued. Then he had lifted his head above the green back of that sofa and seen her. Still, he had not felt any danger to his heart until they'd begun working together, until he'd begun to appreciate her mind and spirit.

Emily Radstock had followed the twists and turns of the case with ease. Alone in that scandalous bedroom, so chilled she nearly shook apart, Em had gone on thinking. She'd seen at once what the letter to Lord Strayde meant, while he had been lost in those other attractions to which he had considered himself immune—creamy skin and swells and hollows of sweet flesh, and a saucy mouth. He had been right to put a check on temptation by sending for Wilde and Miranda.

* * * *

Emily discovered that promising to speak with Lynley and actually speaking with him were two different things. Her first thought about how to reach him was through Phil. As she expected that Roz could use her help with final preparations for the dinner party, she went directly to her sister.

Even in the entry, where a footman greeted her, Emily sensed the bustle of a household preparing for an event, but she found Roz sitting calmly in her pale blue and gold drawing room. She had a sketch of her dining table and a pencil in hand.

"Seating your guests?" Emily glanced over at the great green damask sofa, but did not find Lynley there.

"It's always a delicate matter. If I put Lynley's aunt Silsden on my right, do you think Aunt Mary will be offended?"

Emily studied her sister's sketch. It was pure Roz, thoughtful and correct, but she could see the difficulty of adding Lady Silsden into the usual mix of family and friends.

Roz glanced up. "As she is Lynley's only relation who will attend, I feel that she perhaps deserves some particular notice. There are so many more guests on our side, so to speak."

Emily nodded. A tray of untouched buns and jam sat on the small table next to Roz. "Are you not hungry?" Emily asked.

"Not so much. I feel a little off today. Have a bun if you like."

Emily split a bun, finding it warm inside, and spread some lovely marmalade. "Roz, do you know where Lynley is this morning?"

"Oh, Phil said he left very early, somewhere he had to go."

Emily dropped the bun, which landed jam first on her lap. Her heart beat with quick alarm. It was near eleven. A duel would have taken place at dawn. "Not to meet Ravenhurst?"

Roz looked up from her diagram. "Meet Ravenhurst?"

"Roz, Lady Silsden came to me this morning saying that it's all over London that Lynley and Ravenhurst are to meet."

"In a duel?" Roz frowned. She got up with an effort, one hand pressed to her back, and took a seat at Emily's side. Emily grabbed a spoon from the tea tray and scraped at the jam on her skirt. Her hands shook. She had not expected to love or be loved. Over the years she had grown used to being dismissed by men as too bookish or too outspoken, a woman who wrote letters to the *Times*. She had resolved to be grateful to have her family to love, but she knew that loving them was easy.

Without warning Lynley had appeared in her life, demanding more of her than anyone else, more of her wit, her courage, and her trust. To think he might be gone from her life before she'd begun to spend her unused reserves of love, before she'd become the person she was meant to be, was a prospect so bleak, she did not know how she could endure it.

"Em," Roz said quietly. "Lady Silsden can't be right."

"She can't?"

"No."

"How can you be so sure?"

"Phil. Phil is upstairs at his dressing table. And Lynley would never meet anyone in a duel without Phil as his second. So, you need not worry."

Emily stopped her futile scraping of the jam blotch. Her sister's utter certainty, her confidence in her husband, was an aspect of marriage that changed the ordinary and familiar into something quite profound.

"Did you know that Lynley's father was killed in a duel when his mother ran away with her Russian lover?"

"It must have been excessively painful for Lynley to lose both his parents in that way. That's why I'm glad he has Phil, and now he has you."

But he doesn't have me, Emily thought. *Not the way that Phil has you, not with utter confidence in each other.* Even Emily's parents had that.

Whatever had come over them for that brief interlude in the empty house, he had left her with no assurance of his feelings. There was only the exotic ring on her finger, like something a gypsy fortune-teller might wear, and a memory of kisses and touches that might leave her flesh aching and her heart quite confused.

"Em, I'll have Phil send you a message. I'm sure he knows where Lynley went today."

"Thank you, Roz."

"And don't forget, he has his aunt Silsden," Roz reminded her.

* * * *

When Lynley returned to the club at four, an anxious Wilde greeted him. "The big man's been looking everywhere for you," he said, with a glance at the pistol case under Lynley's arm and the valise in his hand.

"I'd best report then. Can you take these up to my room?"

"Done, sir."

Lynley cast a brief, longing glance at his favorite sofa in the coffee room. He was weary after fighting his own inclinations all day. He headed up the stairs for the big man's office.

If Goldsworthy had been looking for him, then the big man had no idea that Lynley had been to Lyndale and back. He had returned with Sultan and stabled the stallion at Phil's, where the head groom had been more than willing to look after Sultan. Bringing the horse to London was breaking his promise to Goldsworthy, but Lynley thought the spymaster would overlook the transgression when they got results. Besides, Lynley and his horse would be on their way before dawn to find that empty parsonage.

He knocked and entered, and Goldsworthy looked up.

"Ah, lad," the big man said. "Glad you're here. I've had the devil of a time trying to reach you. You have to leave London at once. Take the fastest vehicle you can get. Wilde can go round to the stables for something."

"Where am I going in such a hurry?"

"After Lady Ravenhurst. She's run off."

Lynley took his usual seat opposite the monumental desk.

Goldsworthy frowned. "Can't have any delay, lad. If you leave now, you can pick up the scent. We know the carriage she took, and we know she started on the Dover road."

"Has Ravenhurst gone after her?"

"No. The man's collapsed. He's taken to his bed. But he summoned Chartwell. Ravenhurst thinks the Russians are using his wife as a courier."

"What makes him suspect her?"

"Apparently, she's off to meet Walhouse."

Lynley, of all men, knew that running away with a lover was the desperate act of an unhappy woman. Passion did not make a woman a spy, but it did make her careless of all that she might abandon in her flight—husband, children, and even country.

He rose to his feet. There was less urgency than Goldsworthy supposed. In his pocket Lynley still had the letter he and Emily had found in Walhouse's love nest. Lynley knew precisely where Lady Ravenhurst was going, how long it would take him to get there on Sultan, and what it would cost him to go after her.

It was well that he had met such a woman on the first night of his betrothal to Emily Radstock. Lady Ravenhurst had from the moment of his first observing her reminded him that happiness in marriage was an illusion.

His absence from their engagement party would give Emily Radstock just the excuse she would need to end their false betrothal.

"I'll find her," he said grimly.

Chapter Twenty

The husband hunter who seeks to know only that a gentleman is single mistakes her business. She must cultivate first a more general interest in men, and as husbands come in a variety of types, she must be willing to observe their habits as closely as she observes the habits of the handsomest young lieutenant or most dashing owner of a phaeton and pair. Does she prefer the husband who is a genial host, generally sociable to all he meets, ready to enter into conversation? Does she prefer a man of greater reserve, who may reveal his character only among his most intimate acquaintances? Does she prefer steadiness to passionate volatility? Or dry wit to infectious mirth? The wise husband hunter seeks to understand her preferences before she allows her heart to be engaged.

—The Husband Hunter's Guide to London

By eight nearly twenty close friends and relations had gathered in Roz's drawing room to celebrate Emily and Lynley's engagement. Of the invited guests only Lady Silsden and Lynley had not arrived. His absence was as glaring as the absence of the green damask sofa, which had been pushed into the farthest corner of the room and partially concealed by a linen-draped table topped with a tall blue and white vase. More than once in the past half hour, Em had fixed a smile on her lips as her father looked at his watch and remarked pointedly on her fiancé's tardiness. Her other relatives and friends were content for the moment to mingle and anticipate one of Roz's good suppers.

Emily chatted with friends, reminding herself that a fortnight earlier she hadn't wanted a husband, and she'd felt trapped in an engagement sprung upon her by an unconventional gentleman who lurked behind sofa backs.

She had wanted a husband once, but she acknowledged now, with the wisdom of her nearly twenty-nine years, that what she'd wanted in those first Seasons was not so much a husband as a giddy whirl of experiences and a license to shop for bridal fripperies in all the finest warehouses in London.

The husband's role in this fiction was as her chief admirer. He was an opener of doors, a procurer of ices on hot days, a partner in the waltz, an appreciator of her wit. He had no thoughts or interests that fascinated her or called for her attention. He had no flaws or sorrows that required her sympathy or understanding. His outward attributes were such as would be universally admired by her friends. He needed only to be tall, handsome, and well positioned in the world.

Now, however, because she'd had a chance to glimpse a real man and not the figure of one in her imagination, she recognized the hollowness of her early dream. Lynley's need to move in fashionable society as a spy had turned the tables on her. Tonight she had become the unreal figure, the bride-to-be who was not a woman with real feelings, but a ship's figurehead or a statue come to life.

She straightened her spine and kept her smile in place. It was always good to acquire wisdom even at so late a moment in life as the eve of her twenty-ninth birthday, just a week away. Nothing was better to jettison along life's journey than one's illusions.

She was feeling Lynley's absence because she would miss the spying when they dissolved their engagement, when she announced to the world that they would not suit. But they had one more spy adventure before them. She had been pondering how she and Lynley could contrive an excursion from London into the country to find the empty parsonage. She meant to put the problem before Lynley when they had a moment to themselves.

Her father reached for his watch again, and Emily glanced at Roz. They could wait a few minutes longer, but a dinner party once underway could not easily be put back. Belowstairs everything would be in motion. Timing was the essence of a good dinner. Soups and fish had their moment.

Roz looked calm and attentive to whatever Uncle Walter was saying, but her posture was unnaturally stiff, and she held a hand pressed to the small of her back.

It was a relief a moment later when Gittings announced Lady Silsden. The other guests parted, clearing a little space, into which Lady Silsden staggered, a figure in deep maroon velvet and pale gauze. Someone gasped. Phil stepped forward to offer his hand, but she waved him back. She pressed a palm to her heaving bosom, and drew a shuddering breath, looking around with unseeing eyes.

"What is it, ma'am?" Emily asked.

Lady Silsden's gaze met Emily's. "You've lost him, my dear," she said. "He's run off with Lady Ravenhurst."

It was a blow. Emily would have liked a message, anything rather than being left behind. Hurt said he had played more of a double game than she realized. Maybe all along Lynley's supposed spying had really been about Lady Ravenhurst, with her fragile beauty of the kind that made men rush in to protect and save.

Emily made herself take Lady Silsden's cold hands and help her to a chair. Phil signaled a footman to bring a glass of wine. Roz sank back against the sofa cushions. Phil instantly turned to her, taking her hand and speaking in her ear.

Emily's mind raced. Lynley would not pursue Lady Ravenhurst unless her movement pertained to the case. His betrayal should not wound her feelings so deeply. If he had left London, he betrayed Emily as a partner, not as a lover. He had heard something through the mysterious spymaster he worked for, perhaps.

"Don't you see," Lady Silsden pleaded. "He's repeating his father's folly. You must send someone after him. He must be stopped."

"I believe that's my office," said Emily's father quietly. "No rogue jilts my daughter."

"Father, wait," Emily said. "We don't even know that Lynley has left London." She glanced at Phil. "Do we?"

Phil looked sheepish. "He brought Sultan up from the country today. I'll send to the stables to inquire if the horse is still there."

Emily's common sense reasserted itself. Lynley might pretend to be an imbecile, but of all the men she knew, he was the least capable of folly. She wondered who was circulating such nonsense. She encouraged Lady Silsden to drink her wine. "Now, ma'am, you must tell me how you heard this disturbing news."

"It was that daughter of my friend, Lady Throckmorton. She sent me a message. She heard from Lord Barksted that Ravenhurst has taken to his bed."

Emily wanted to laugh and cry at once. Sophia Throckmorton and Lord Barksted, a pair as indifferent to truth as the worst of London gossips, the one out of giddiness, the other, out of malice.

Phil, standing at his wife's side, cleared his throat. "We'll get to the bottom of this." He looked around the room. "You don't know Lynley, but I do. He would never serve my sister-in-law such a turn as this. I regret that we must delay our celebration of the betrothal, but we can delay dinner no longer. Please, let us eat."

Gittings appeared and threw open the doors, and gentlemen began to lead their ladies to the dining room. Roz looked up at Phil with shining eyes. He helped her to her feet. She took a step and froze, clutching his arm, her eyes wide in surprise and shock. She shuddered and took a gasping breath.

"Roz?" Phil asked.

"Oh dear," she said. "I believe my pains have started."

"Shall we send for the doctor?" Phil asked.

"I'll go," said their father.

Roz shook her head and reached out a hand to Emily. "Stop. I have Emily."

Emily took her sister's arm. "And," she said, "we have Aunt Sarah with us."

Roz smiled. "Let her have her dinner, and then send her up to me. I think it may be hours yet."

"Of course," said Phil. "Hours."

* * * *

A cold wind blew, and shadows of clouds passing over the face of the moon made for a shifting, uncertain landscape. In spite of their journey earlier in the day, Sultan kept a steady pace. Lady Ravenhurst, traveling post, had stopped once to change horses. He and Sultan were perhaps two hours behind her and gaining as the weather grew bitter. He would not think of the dinner he was missing, or the embarrassment his absence would cause Em. Loving her had not been part of the plan, but with each outrageous thing she did, with each step as she followed his lead, he'd found himself in deeper. He had not really recognized what was happening until he'd pulled Barksted's henchman from her back. It would be some satisfaction to find the papers and be done with the case he had shared with her.

Lynley found the parsonage of St. Agatha's screened from the road by a stand of chestnuts and firs a couple of hundred yards from the church itself. A gravel carriage sweep passed in an arc in front of a plain, two-story, yellow stone house. From the road no light appeared, but a hint of smoke drifted on the wind to suggest that someone had lit a fire inside.

Lynley rode beyond the parsonage into the churchyard, dismounted and led Sultan round to the back of the church. He settled the stallion in a sheltered corner where the transept crossed the nave, made a couple of adjustments to his attire, and loaded his pistol. Every instinct told him that he had done the right thing in leaving Emily Radstock behind.

He approached the parsonage cautiously, choosing his ground to avoid giving any alarm from the sound of footsteps on gravel. A horse nickered from an outbuilding at the back of the house. Lynley stopped and waited several minutes. No one emerged, and the only sounds from inside came from horses, a pair of them, he thought. He opened the door and found a neat curricle hitched to a pair of bays. Someone was ready to leave.

He turned to the parsonage, passing through a little walled garden in the rear. Thin bars of light fell through a half-closed curtain over a bow window. He crept closer and looked in through the crack. The room appeared to be a study, lined with empty bookcases.

In front of a low fire a young man with golden hair and a strong resemblance to Allegra Walhouse sat facing another person hidden by the wings of an armchair. The man leaned forward, speaking to his companion in what appeared to be a savage manner.

Lynley saw no sign of weapons or servants. Time for the highwayman to make an appearance.

He circled the house and found a door in the front that opened directly on an empty parlor. From the parlor a passage led to the back of the house. He could hear the heated conversation as he stepped quietly along the passage, listening for any sign that he'd been detected. The study door was open, and Lynley paused to listen.

"You promised to take me away," a plaintive female voice said. Lynley recognized the hurt voice as Lady Ravenhurst's. She must be the party in the wing chair.

"What did you think we would live on?" the young man answered bitterly. "Your baubles?"

Lynley stepped into the shadows at the back of the room, pistol in hand. "I believe that's my cue," he said.

The young man jumped to his feet, his back to the fire. "Who the bloody hell are you?"

Lady Ravenhurst started. Lynley observed that although she was dressed for travel in a warm cloak and half boots, her hands and feet were bound, and a stout coil of rope secured her to the chair. A purple bruise on one cheekbone suggested that she had been beaten into accepting her bonds.

A brief spurt of rage passed through him. Apparently, in addition to betraying his country, the man meant to betray his lover. The lady's situation was a complication Lynley had not foreseen. A fleeting thought that what he needed at the moment was Emily Radstock's help passed in and out of his mind. He was alone.

"It's customary," Lynley said, subduing his anger, "in my line of work to relieve ladies of their baubles and gentlemen of their purses. As traffic is slow on the road tonight, I thought to try my luck here."

The young man affected composure, but looked closely at Lynley's pistol. It was the gun he'd wished he'd had at fourteen when his mother's lover had laughed in his face. Its curved stock fit in Lynley's hand. The adjustable hair trigger, roller bearings, gold-lined touchhole, waterproof pan, and patent breech made it a formidable weapon.

"A highwayman, are you? Have some baubles then and be off with you," the young man suggested. He gestured toward two traveling cases that stood next to the door directly in Lynley's path. Lynley glanced at the cases, noting that the trim and fittings marked one as belonging to a female.

"And leave a lady in such obvious distress?" Lynley moved closer without leaving the shadows. "As courtesy to ladies is the first principle of the highwayman's code, I must ask you to untie your companion."

"Well, I won't," said the young man mulishly. "She's tied up for her own good."

"Clive," Lady Ravenhurst cried. "Don't leave me." She stared at him with wide, pleading eyes. She had the sort of delicate helpless beauty to which, Lynley knew, many men were drawn. His mother had had that sort of beauty.

"You must enlighten, me, Walhouse—it is Walhouse, isn't it?—as to the advantage to the lady of being abandoned and bound in an unoccupied house. Are the cloak and boots to keep her warm when you're gone?"

"Who the devil are you?" Walhouse kept his gaze on Lynley. "I'm not the villain here. Barksted is. He hounded her into this mad flight. No doubt her dolt of a husband is on his way."

"Eager to wash your hands of her, are you? Your horses are ready, Walhouse. You may leave as soon as you release the lady."

"I told you, it is better for her to be found tied up." Walhouse sent a calculating glance toward the two cases and the door. There was a cold, contemptuous cast to his features. Lynley had seen that look before on the face of his mother's lover. It was the look of a man who believed women to be the natural prey of men.

"Then we are at an impasse, I fear," said Lynley.

"Oh very well, but you're making a mull of the whole thing." Walhouse turned to Lady Ravenhurst and began to undo the rope binding her to the chair.

"Clive," she said, "you were going to take me to Paris."

He pulled ruthlessly at her bound hands. "Only if you kept your end of the bargain," he said bitterly.

"My end," she cried. "I sent your gloves. Where could I send your other things? Your coat, your hat? Archer told me you were nowhere to be found. I didn't hear from you."

"Hush. Not another word. You'll hang for treason if you're not careful." Walhouse pulled the last rope free from Lady Ravenhurst's feet.

"Treason?" She looked at him with shocked awareness. "Ravenhurst's papers. It was you. You stole them. You used me."

"Ah, Pamela. Those papers were part of your charm. You're expensive, you know, and your gaming debts had to be paid."

Lady Ravenhurst shrank at the cruel words. "You deceived me. I depended on you."

"Oh come, no harm done. You've had an adventure. You can go back to Ravenhurst, or you could before this fellow's interference. You were better off tied up."

"Go, Walhouse," said Lynley. "You're done here."

Walhouse shrugged. At the door he reached for his case.

"Leave it," Lynley ordered, his pistol leveled at Walhouse.

"Clive!" It was an anguished cry, and it made Walhouse check for an instant.

Lady Ravenhurst jumped up and threw herself after her departing lover, her feet tangling in her cloak. Lynley reached to arrest her fall, catching her by one arm. Walhouse seized his traveling case. Lynley just had time to fire. The doorframe splintered. Walhouse shrieked and then was gone.

The lady collapsed, sobbing at Lynley's feet. He stuffed the spent pistol in his coat pocket and let her weep until there came a brief drumming of horses' hooves and a rattling of wheels on the road.

"He's gone," Lynley said. "Come, there's an inn nearby where you can be safe and decide what you wish to do."

He lifted her from the floor and led her through the passage to a door at the back of the house.

"My case," she said, turning back just as he opened the door on the dark night.

"We'll send for it," Lynley said. He would not burden Sultan.

The wind had grown stronger, the clouds heavier, and the air noticeably colder. Lady Ravenhurst shivered at Lynley's side. The missing papers were no doubt on their way to Dover, but Lynley did not think Walhouse would get far. His shriek revealed that either the bullet or a wood fragment had winged him, and the worsening weather would compel him to stop before he reached Dover. Once Lynley had seen to the lady's comfort and security, he would continue the pursuit. Sultan was a match for any pair of horses in England.

"Come," he urged again.

"You have no sensibility, do you?" she asked.

"None," he agreed, pulling her after him into the night. She was right. Her inability to see her lover for what he was had worn out Lynley's sympathy.

Beneath the rush of the wind in the trees, he heard the unmistakable clatter of a heavier vehicle turning onto the gravel sweep of the parsonage.

"Someone's here," Lady Ravenhurst cried.

Lynley pulled her along the rough path in the dark, the wind tugging at their garments.

Two men erupted from the rear of the house. One of them held a lantern aloft. Its beam caught Lynley and Lady Ravenhurst as they neared the garden wall.

"Found 'er, Lord Barksted," a voice shouted.

Lady Ravenhurst gave a cry and turned to look back at the house.

"Hey there, you. Stop," the rough voice called.

Lynley kept going, but his companion stumbled. He halted, turning to lift her up. As he rose, a shot cracked, and a bullet plowed into his right arm just below the shoulder. He lost his hold on the lady, and she sank into the grass with a sob.

"Not another step, mind," said the rough voice. "I've got another popper loaded."

Barksted appeared in the doorway at the rear of the house. "Lady Ravenhurst," he said, stepping into the garden, accompanied by the man holding the lantern. "And who have we here? Some dastardly rogue who's abducted you, my dear?"

Barksted signaled the man with the lantern to hold it higher, and the beam caught Lynley.

Barksted's face contorted in an ugly grin of satisfaction. "Lynley. The man who always interferes with my plans."

Lynley held himself as straight as he could. He had a spent pistol and a right arm that was rapidly becoming useless. "Merely assisting the lady in returning to her husband."

Barksted appeared to think. "What a trying ordeal you've had, my lady," he said. "Shall we put it about that you were abducted by this rogue? I think that story will serve admirably."

He came forward and extended a hand to lift Lady Ravenhurst up. She cast one helpless look at Lynley and took Barksted's hand.

"I've a coach waiting. Let's return you to your husband."

It was a moment Lynley knew well, and he tasted the full bitterness of the lesson he'd failed to learn as a boy, that a man could not separate a woman from her folly.

Barksted and Lady Ravenhurst reached the back of the house, when he turned to his henchmen. "He's yours, boys," he said. To Lynley, he added, "You were warned."

In an instant they were on him. He was no match for them without the use of his right arm. He did his best to protect his head and ribs from the blows.

In two minutes it was over. Barksted whistled, and with one last kick at Lynley's side, his henchmen withdrew.

Lynley lay in the grass at the back of the garden until he heard the carriage pull out of the gravel sweep, onto the road. He rolled to his knees and pushed himself up with his left hand. Dizziness troubled him briefly. The wind had died. Low clouds covered the sky. He staggered through the garden gate and whistled for Sultan. His usually piercing whistle sounded feeble in his ears.

But the horse came. Lynley draped his good arm over Sultan's withers and let the horse support him. Sultan gave an anxious snort at the smell of blood, but settled down to walk with Lynley toward the outbuilding where Walhouse had kept his carriage and pair. The first wet flakes of spring snow fell as they neared the doors.

Inside there would be hay, old hay, but hay and a roof over their heads. Lynley told Sultan to stand in a makeshift stall that smelled of dry hay. He leaned against the stall partition and stripped off his neckcloth. He wadded it up and stuffed it against the wound in his arm. Then he slid down into the old hay, pulling his cloak around him. Sultan leaned down and nuzzled Lynley's head. Just a little rest and they'd be on their way.

"Wait for me, boy," Lynley whispered.

Chapter Twenty-One

*Fatal to the husband hunter's future happiness is any
inclination to romanticize men. The husband hunter must
refrain from expecting her fellow creatures to act as if they
stepped from the pages of chivalric tales or stirring romances.
She must do so not out of the selfish motive of protecting herself
from disillusionment, but rather from the generous motive of
freeing herself to see the gentlemen in her life as the mortal
beings they truly are.*

—*The Husband Hunter's Guide to London*

At eleven it became clear that Roz's baby was determined to make an
entrance into the world that night. A heavy wet snow had begun to fall.
Emily sent express messages to her mother and brother. Her father and
Phil saw their guests off and retired to the drawing room.

On the advice of Aunt Sarah, summoned at the end of dinner, Roz
walked up and down her room for several hours, stopping to breathe
through the pains, until her labor entered a new, more intense phase. Aunt
Sarah then directed housemaids in the preparation of the bed for birthing.
They moved Roz to the bed, fed her pieces of ice, and helped her through
the cresting waves of pain.

Emily held Roz's hand, marveling at her sister's endurance. Roz, who
had seemed so delicate, showed a strength Emily had not imagined a
woman could possess.

Aunt Sarah put a sturdy arm around Emily's shoulder and gave a squeeze. "The body has its own wisdom, if we will but heed its messages," she said. "Roz's body will take over now, and lead her."

The doctor came from an evening engagement some time after one, shaking snow from his hat and coat, and praising their efforts. He pronounced everything going according to Nature's plan. Emily had a thought or two on Nature's plan and how it seemed disproportionately demanding of women, but she ran back and forth to her father and Phil, reporting Roz's progress.

At five, as pale early light brightened the windows, a silver, shimmering little boy, slippery as a fish, and fair and mild as Roz herself, entered the world and gave his first lusty cry. A tearful Roz reached to hold him close at once and called for Phil.

She was made to wait while Aunt Sarah and the doctor supervised all that must be done for baby and mother. To Emily's surprise, as the signs of birthing were whisked away, Roz, too, shed her pains, as if she had not spent the last hours sweating and shaking, red of face and dropping from weariness. The great effort that had overtaken her body had passed. The storm had faded in joy. Her face was radiant as the brightest day after the clouds cleared.

When admitted to her chamber, Phil climbed onto the bed next to his wife and put his arm around her as she held the babe. He slipped a finger into his son's tiny grasp, and they sat stunned and wondering at the life their love had made.

At seven Emily returned to Candover House to change and go in search of her love.

* * * *

The snow was already melting and turning the streets to mush when Emily banged on the door of the chemist's shop in Bond Street so proudly named by Miranda Kirby. Persistent knocking and pressing of the bell eventually drew Miranda to the window. When she saw Emily, she opened the shop door.

"Miss, come in out of the chill. Whatever brings you here at this time?"

Emily stepped inside, rubbing her cold hands together. "I need your help to find Lynley."

"My help, miss?"

"You and your betrothed know the spymaster, don't you?"

Miranda colored brightly, but closed the shop door with a bang. "But, miss, you're not to know about the spies or Mr. Goldsworthy."

"Mr. Goldsworthy, is it?" Emily asked. "Take me to him."

"Oh, miss, you have no idea what you're asking." Miranda twisted the ends of a blue shawl in her hands.

"What about your young man, Mr. Wilde? Will he take me to Goldsworthy?"

Miranda took a breath. "Good idea, miss. I'll fetch Nate. You wait right here."

Miranda disappeared through a pair of crimson velvet curtains at the rear of the shop, and Emily heard her footsteps hurrying down a passageway. A door opened and closed somewhere at the back of the building.

Emily looked round the little shop with its orderly arrangement of jars and tins of lotions and salves. The place smelled of citrus, lavender, and deeper, muskier scents. She lifted a jar of lotion from the shelf, and raised it to her nose. It smelled of almonds. The label claimed the most amazing results from the regular application of the lotion inside, and it occurred to her that she already possessed a powerful means of persuasion should the spymaster resist her plan to rescue Lynley.

Goldsworthy's name was the key to the bold idea that had sprung into her head. She knew exactly how to move him to help her in the manner in which she wished to be helped. He would resist. It would be just like a man to pat her on the head and send her off and claim that he would take care of the situation. But women, whose bodies men disdained as soft and weak, were stronger than men ever gave them credit for being.

She replaced the lotion on the shelf and went around behind the shop counter. In a drawer under the counter she found just the pen, ink, and paper she was looking for. She began to write, though the ink was cold and the pen, badly mended. The words came rapidly.

She had much more to say, but the distant door at the rear of the shop banged again, and voices raised in argument came her way. She put down her pen, shook the paper dry, and folded the sheet. Miranda and Wilde stepped through the crimson curtains.

"Good morning, miss. What's this Miranda is saying about your wanting to see Mr. Goldsworthy?" He frowned at Miranda.

"Good morning, Mr. Wilde. Do not blame Miranda for my actions. You must be aware that Lynley left town yesterday, and that he has not returned."

"Sir Ajax is well able to handle himself, miss," Wilde said through tight lips.

"I'm sure. Nevertheless. He is mortal, and he may not have anticipated certain complications in this case. I want you to take me to Mr. Goldsworthy, who if nothing else, has a duty to look after his own."

"Mr. Goldsworthy," said Wilde, "doesn't like to make himself known to...the world, miss. Keeps to himself, he does." For a moment the posh accent slipped, and the young man sounded as if he came from the poorest of London streets.

"I'm sure he doesn't, Mr. Wilde, but if he does not see me this morning, he can expect to be widely known to the public by the end of the week, for I intend to expose him to the *Times* for what he is—a spymaster in our midst." Emily held up the paper on which she'd written her letter.

"Miss, you wouldn't," protested Miranda.

"I will."

Wilde's expression grew obstinate, while Miranda looked panicked.

Emily tried a different tactic. "Really, you two, didn't Lynley rescue you recently, and now you refuse to let me rescue him?"

"But, miss," said Wilde, "Sir Ajax has his pistols and his black horse."

"Oh," said Miranda, "he's playing the highwayman, miss. He is quite... daunting in his black cape and hat with his pistol pointing at a body."

"And he's a crack shot," added Wilde.

"Fearsome, is he?" she asked.

Two heads nodded vigorously.

"It's a disguise, you know," she said. She would not tell them, but she understood the disguise. Some part of Lynley was still the boy who had failed to save his parents from their folly. No matter how tall and strong he'd become since the moment when the Russian soldier had struck him down, he needed the highwayman's disguise to look dangerous. "Take me to Goldsworthy." She held up her letter.

A long moment passed. Emily stood as still and unwavering as a marble column. At last Miranda tugged at Wilde's sleeve and turned imploring eyes up to him, and the youth yielded. Emily stuffed the letter into the little reticule on her wrist.

"Wilde," she said, "Miranda can show me the way. If you know how Mr. Goldsworthy likes to travel, can you send for a vehicle and horses?"

Emily thought she had gone almost too far, but Wilde nodded. He held open the crimson curtains, and Miranda led the way into a narrow passage. They left the shop, crossed a patch of garden, newly green with blades of grass, and entered the kitchen of a building that must, Emily realized, have its front on Albemarle Street.

Wilde left them at some stairs and Miranda led Emily up to a door on the second story. With a quick intake of breath, Miranda summoned her resolve and rapped on the door.

"Mr. Goldsworthy, someone to see you," she said.

A deep voice rumbled, "Enter."

Emily took hold of the knob, and Miranda fled.

The room she entered had a military feel to it with canvas draping two walls, maps and cabinets along another, and in the center a desk, which, she felt sure, was larger than any of the cages at the Exeter Change.

Mr. Goldsworthy was built on the scale of Chunee, but russet and brown in hue with a great shaggy head and beard. He was like some craggy oak tree in the wood. She understood at once why Wilde and Miranda had resisted bringing her to him.

She strode into the room, took a stand before the great desk, and met the man's startled gaze at her boldness.

"Miss, you can't be here," he said.

Emily stepped forward. The huge desk was taller than her waist. "But here I am. And what's more, you need my help."

"Your help?" The bushy brows shot up. "Who are you?"

"Emily Radstock. I'm here to rescue Lynley." She plucked a pen from the desk.

"Lynley?"

"Sir Ajax Lynley, my betrothed, who has gone after Clive Walhouse and Ravenhurst's missing papers." She refused to believe that he'd run away with Lady Ravenhurst. "What's more, unless you are willing to act at once, there is a very good chance that Lynley's mission will fail. And I won't have him sacrificed to your indifference as Malikov was."

The big man gave her an assessing look. "You seem to know a good deal about matters that are not proper to your sphere, miss."

"My sphere? You mean the sphere of any subject of His Majesty with a care for the safety and security of Britain?" Emily waved the pen she'd picked up.

He watched the pen's movement, suspicious of her intent.

"If you refuse to help me, Mr. Goldsworthy, do not suppose that I will not mount a rescue mission on my own, and do know that the following letter will appear in the *Times* if I do not return with Lynley, whole and sound, within three days."

Emily dropped the pen and pulled the letter she'd begun from her reticule. She read the opening she had composed, and then she improvised. She knew what would come next.

"Sir:

"It has come to the attention of this writer that foreign agents of the most dangerous sort operate in the midst of London, moving among His Majesty's ordinary subjects with impunity, promoting the aims of Britain's enemies through espionage and murder.

"In recent months such agents have procured vital Foreign Office documents for the benefit of our enemies and have reached into the most secure of London prisons to murder one of their own to prevent his disclosures. What became of Thomas Culley in the Fleet?

"Furthermore, the public should know that the government employs English spies to combat this enemy, and that these spies are granted broad license to burgle and spy and coerce. The ordinary person may wonder how such spies could operate without gaining notice. He or she should look again at certain chemists' shops and clubs, which act as fronts for the nests of spies among us."

"Stop." Goldsworthy held up one of his great hands. "You must not send that letter under any circumstances."

"Then you'll accompany me to find Lynley?" Emily held her breath. Goldsworthy appeared as immovable as a craggy boulder jutting out of a hillside.

"It's all well and good for you to insist, but we've no idea where he's gone."

Emily let her lips curve upward in a triumphant smile. "I know exactly where he's gone."

Chapter Twenty-Two

Even when the husband hunter feels most secure of the gentleman to whom she has pledged herself, she must expect quarrels to be a part of her intercourse with him, for we are flawed creatures, likely to wound one another out of our own past hurts and disappointments. Outwardly there may be no sign of the inward scars we bear, but if our love for one another is to prosper, we must confess our errors and resolve to love in a new way.

—The Husband Hunter's Guide to London

Mr. Goldsworthy, in spite of his bulk, moved nimbly and decisively. In half an hour he and Emily were seated in a curricle behind a pair of sturdy horses with Wilde in the groom's position at the rear. Emily had had time to pen a brief note to her father. The melting snow threw up slush and mud as they rolled out of London. A cold, sharp wind blew the sky empty of cloud.

Until they stopped for a change of horses, Emily refused to confide the location of the empty parsonage and her reason for believing it to be Lynley's destination as well as that of Walhouse. As they waited in the coffee room of a small posting inn for the new team to be put to their carriage, a stir at the inn door caught Emily's attention. She froze at the sound of a familiar voice. At Goldsworthy's side, she leaned back to let the big man's bulk conceal her.

"Barksted," she whispered.

Goldsworthy looked over at the newcomers standing in the entry with the landlord. "And Lady Ravenhurst," he said.

Emily ventured a glance around Goldsworthy's massive girth. Lady Ravenhurst clung to Barksted's arm, looking haggard and disheveled, and yet still lovely, while Barksted made demands of the innkeeper. He asked for a maid for the lady, and commanded a private room. The hostess came and led Lady Ravenhurst upstairs. And Barksted disappeared with the landlord.

"Give me ten minutes," Emily told Goldsworthy. She had not realized until she saw Lady Ravenhurst's beauty how even she, who had come to know Lynley as much as he permitted anyone to know him, could doubt him.

Upstairs, a maid bringing a basin and a pitcher of hot water showed Emily to the door. Emily knocked and a tremulous voice admitted her.

Lady Ravenhurst sat looking helplessly at a hand mirror, her golden hair falling down one side of her face, a silver brush in her hand.

"You," she said.

"Where's Lynley?" Emily asked.

"Oh." Lady Ravenhurst turned the silver brush over in her hands, not meeting Emily's eye. "Barksted will not want me to tell."

"You must, however," Emily insisted, trying to keep the outrage from her voice.

The lady appeared to engage in an inner struggle. "Oh, very well," she said. "He's at that parsonage on the road to Longfield."

Emily was tempted to turn on her heel and leave at once, but she asked, "He's not gone to Dover?"

"Dover? Where traitors go?" she said bitterly. "No."

"And you? Where is Barksted taking you?" Emily could see a purple bruise on Lady Ravenhurst's cheek.

"Back to Ravenhurst," she said in a small voice. It was an admission of defeat, and Emily had no comfort to offer.

"Thank you," Emily said, and turned for the door. She no longer envied Lady Ravenhurst her fragile beauty.

"Wait," said the lady. "You should know. One of Barksted's men shot him."

Everything stopped for a moment. Emily's lungs forgot to take their next breath. Her heart forgot to beat. Her hand refused to turn the doorknob. "Is he dead?" she asked.

Lady Ravenhurst shook her head. "I don't think so."

* * * *

Emily knew that the distance to Longfield would be counted nothing on a fair day with a decent pair of horses and a well-sprung vehicle, but melting snow and gnawing worry made the way long and tedious. Goldsworthy made his displeasure known that she had not asked Lady Ravenhurst about Walhouse. At a crossroads Wilde jumped down to ask directions of a passing farmer, and then they were there, driving past a stand of chestnut trees onto the gravel sweep, pulling up to the plain yellow house.

No one answered Goldsworthy's call when they entered. The house smelled of damp and cold fires. Emily glanced at the empty rooms as she passed toward an open door at the end of the passage. A walled garden and a small field lay between the parsonage and a sort of barn, its doors hanging open. Behind her Goldsworthy tramped about while Wilde bounded up the stairs. She lifted her skirts and descended into the garden. A squat stone church with a square Norman tower stood off to one side. In the trampled grass at the base of the garden wall she found a pistol and a smear of blood in a patch of snow.

"Lynley," she shouted, scanning the field.

From within the little barn, a horse whinnied, and Emily took off at a run. The snow had retreated, making islands of white in a sea of green. She stumbled her way over the rough ground, her skirts growing wet and muddy. She stepped through the open barn door, peering into the gloom and feeling the deeper cold where no sun had penetrated. The little barn smelled of neglect, of rank hay and old dung. Three stalls lined the wall to her left. Dust-covered tools and tack hung on the wall to her right.

At first she thought she'd imagined the horse's whinny. Then a magnificent black head rose above the second stall. The great black horse shook himself all over. He was saddled and bridled. For a heart-wrenching moment she could not breathe. Lynley would never leave a horse untended.

"Hello," she said, approaching slowly, wishing she had an apple or some hay. "Hello, Sultan."

The horse's ears flicked toward her at the sound of his name. "Where's Lynley?" Emily asked. "Where's your master?"

She slipped into the stall and extended her hand to let the horse know she offered no danger. She stroked the long neck. "You've been here too long, haven't you, Sultan? Let me find Lynley, and I'll see to you."

She stepped back from the horse, trying to gather her wits. Lynley had not returned to the house. She had seen no sign of him in the field. Her mind raced with plans to retrace her steps through the grass and call Wilde, when glancing down, she saw a long, low heap of black clothes, lying like a mound of turned-up earth in a field, from which a pair of muddied boots protruded.

She ducked around the front of the horse and dropped to her knees in the old straw. Lynley lay rolled in a black cloak against the side of the stall, his eyes closed, his face drawn and white, a thin line of dried blood at the corner of his mouth. She put a hand to his rough cheek. He shivered but did not open his eyes.

She leaned down and kissed his cold lips. She whispered, "Later, my love, I will be very angry with you."

She pulled herself up, offered the horse a reassuring word and a stroke on the silky neck, and strode for the house.

Goldsworthy stood in the back doorway. "Well?" he shouted.

"I found Lynley. He's hurt, and we need to get him to the house."

"Did he get the papers?"

"He's wounded," Emily replied, governing her temper.

Wilde appeared and squeezed past Goldsworthy. In the barn the youth and the horse regarded each other warily. Emily moved Sultan to a second stall. With Wilde's help, she roused Lynley. His eyes fluttered open. He looked straight at Wilde. "Walhouse has the papers. Cannot have got far. Winged him," he said.

Emily reminded herself that she could berate him later for his single-mindedness. "Where are you hurt?" she asked him.

"Em?" He seemed baffled by her presence. "Shot. Arm," he said through gritted teeth.

"Then let's take care of that," she said. "Mr. Goldsworthy can go after the papers."

Lynley gave her one more puzzled look, then nodded. Together, she and Wilde got him to sit upright and offered him coffee from a flask Wilde carried. The journey across the field, through the garden, and into a wingchair in the cold parlor at the back of the house further tried Emily's patience.

She set Wilde to work making a fire and searching the house for anything of use like bedding, candles, and water, while she helped Lynley out of his heavy cloak and mud-caked boots. His stockinged feet were icy cold, and she wrapped them in her cloak. The room warmed as they worked, and whenever Mr. Goldsworthy grumbled at the delay, Emily reminded him of her letter. She made Wilde promise to stop at the first inn they passed to send for a doctor.

When, at last, though it could not have taken long, Emily had what she needed, she let them go.

She looked around the small parlor with its once cheery red sprig wallpaper, somewhat battered white wainscot, and bare plank floors, and laughed. Of all the places for a woman to be compromised by her lover, this one was woefully lacking in the elements of a successful seduction. A sadly banged-up copper kettle simmered on the grate. An overturned box held a pair of chipped cups and a tea jar with a few faint leaves. Slanting late afternoon light came through the north-facing windows. It was no love nest where she and Lynley could fall into a sumptuous bed hung with silks and piled high with soft cushions.

She turned to Lynley and found him watching her.

"You've been busy," he said, his voice low and a bit unsteady.

"You have no idea." She crossed to stand in front of him, her skirts against his knees, looking down on the tousled hair, the dark shadow of his beard against the pallor of his skin, and the furrow of pain between his brows.

"A number of things puzzle me," he said.

"You're surprised to see me here?"

"With Goldsworthy."

"Ah," she said. "Your spymaster did need some persuading."

"No doubt you'll explain it all to me." She heard the weariness in his voice.

"I will, my love," she said, "but now, we really must get you out of these clothes."

A light flared in his dark eyes. With his good hand, he pulled Emily to stand between his knees, closing them against her legs to hold her in place. His shirt collar gaped open above the black silk of his waistcoat.

"What did you do with your neckcloth?" she asked. She reached for the top button of his waistcoat and began to work the tiny buttons down his chest.

"Stuffed it over the bullet hole." With his good hand he indicated a bulge in his right sleeve.

"Very wise," she said, releasing the last button of his waistcoat and gently spreading it open over the fine lawn shirt. "Can you lift your left arm?"

He complied with a grin, and she pulled his coat sleeve up until he could free his arm.

"Lean forward," she ordered.

He did, pressing his forehead into the hollow of her throat where the lace collar dipped, breathing against her skin. For a moment they leaned against each other, like spent runners catching a ragged breath. She peeled the close-fitting coat from his back until only the right sleeve remained. He inhaled sharply.

"This part may hurt," she said, easing the shirt off his shoulder. His eyes closed briefly, and then opened as she slid the coat over the injured arm. The bloodied neckcloth tumbled free, and Emily caught it.

His lawn shirt stuck to his arm. Blood had spilled and stained the shirt from a small hole no bigger than Emily's thumb, an angry circle of singed black fibers. A similar hole marked the bullet's exit.

"Wilde promised he would send a doctor from the next inn," she told him, studying the way the shirt stuck to his flesh.

"How long do you think we have?" he asked.

The question sent a flash of heat through her. At least Lynley would not die of a chill. She took a steadying breath and gently pulled free of his legs. Spreading his ruined coat on the floor, she stepped onto it, lifted her skirts and reached for the ties on her petticoats.

He grinned. "This is promising," he said.

She laughed. "I'm just being practical."

"I'm not allowed to hope for more?" he asked, one brow raised.

"Clean bandages," she said, giving a little shimmy and letting her petticoats settle onto his coat. She stepped out of them and whisked them up onto the other chair. She managed after several tries to tear a strip of cloth. She poured hot water from the kettle into one of the chipped cups and soaked her makeshift bandage, then wrapped the wet strip around his arm.

"I should have had you with me," he confessed.

"I did think we were partners," she said.

"I was strongly opposed to Barksted's bullyboys or anyone else putting hands on you again."

"I feel quite the same way about Barksted's henchmen banging you up. This," she said, waving a hand vaguely over his person, "belongs to me." In time she would kiss every inch of him.

"I can make it up to you," he said.

"I'm interested."

When she judged that the wet compress had had sufficient time to do its work, she lifted it from his arm. Gently, she peeled his shirt away from the skin, pleased to see that the blackened fibers remained attached to the torn shirt and the wound itself had only a little black residue around the edge. She put aside the stained compress.

"Now, your waistcoat and shirt."

"You won't stop until you have me naked, will you?"

"I do like the idea of you naked, but I suspect the doctor will only need to see your arm."

She made him stand briefly to get the waistcoat off and pull his shirttails free of his trousers. He was a bit wobbly on his legs, so she pushed him gently back down into the chair. She undid his cuffs and worked the shirt off his uninjured side and over his head before pulling it from the wounded arm.

She held the linen, warm from his body, and stared at what she'd uncovered. She wanted to run her hands over the fine broad shoulders, and down the chest with its swells of muscle and swirls of soft dark hair to the taut belly. The bullet had passed through a bulge of arm muscle just below his shoulder. Blue and yellow bruises marked his ribs and torso.

"Barksted's men," he said, watching her.

She nodded. They had wounded his flesh, but the faint line on his imperfect mouth was the real wound, the old hurt that had sent him off alone to rescue a woman who didn't wish to be rescued. Emily traced it with her finger. He shivered under her touch.

"You may wonder," he said, "that I came to Lady Ravenhurst's assistance when I should simply have taken the papers and been on my way. Had I found Walhouse alone, I would have done just that."

Emily waited, holding her breath, stilling every judgment.

He released a long, shaky breath. "When my mother left, I thought I could stop her. I pleaded and argued. I tried to fight her lover to keep her with us, with my father and me. She wept, but she watched him beat me."

Emily had wanted him naked, but this was more, this baring of the hurt he kept concealed behind his cool, bored indifference. She wanted to tell him that he had been young, that she knew what it was to be young and to imagine that you could right wrongs in the world by your own valiant efforts.

"You aren't that boy anymore. You are wiser, and better armed."

He laughed. "But still wrong." He looked at her, his dark eyes filled with honesty and something more. "I was wrong yesterday again, wrong to try to stop her...alone. I should have waited to bring my partner with me—you, Em."

It was an unlikely admission, an admission of need. Lynley, she realized, had been determined to need no one from the time of the disaster. His aunt called it a disaster because it involved the family in scandal, but the real disaster had been the grave injury to the heart of a loving boy. His aunt and his uncle had completed the work begun by his mother and her lover until he had refused to be vulnerable or open.

Emily dropped his ruined shirt and leaned over to kiss him. With his good hand he pulled her down into his lap and settled her against the unhurt shoulder. She pressed against him and placed her hand on his heart, a heart that could now heal.

But as she felt its steady beat, she was tempted to move her hand over his chest, to fill her senses with the textures of his skin, the rough and smooth, the taut ridges of muscle, the soft swirls of hair, and the flat coins of his nipples. He was sensitive there, and when she felt his body flex in response to her touch, she smiled, her lips brushing his collarbone.

She owed him this. He had, after all, been teasing her senses for days, awakening yearnings she had not felt before.

"Are you seducing me?" he asked.

"Is it working?"

He nodded wordlessly, and Emily continued the explorations that seemed more likely than any saline draft to distract him from the pain of his wounded arm.

Chapter Twenty-Three

*What numbers of girls are turned out in London each
Season, dressed and coiffed with the elegance their families'
means allow, feeling only that they must attract the notice
of gentlemen around them and that it is the duty of those
gentlemen to choose a wife? The husband hunter must not be
like one of these—ignorant of human nature and unacquainted
with her own heart, lacking a plan of action and with no sense
of her duty to shape her destiny. To become a woman, she must
act. She must choose. Unless she takes charge of her life, she
remains, though a wife, a perpetual girl.*

—*The Husband Hunter's Guide to London*

The doctor came near dusk as the sky grew pale and the trees turned
to black rustling shadows. Mr. Windle was a bewhiskered gentleman in
an old-fashioned brown coat, with a brusque manner.

He hollered a greeting from the door, and at Emily's reply, he tromped
into the little parlor.

"What's this I hear about a man who's been shot?" he asked, coming
to a halt in front of Lynley, his bag in his hand.

Lynley pulled aside the coat he'd been using for warmth.

Windle's eyes widened at the sight of the bullet hole. "Bring that light
closer, miss," he ordered.

Emily stood holding their one candle over Lynley. Mr. Windle peered
at the bullet wound and then at the bruises on Lynley's chest and ribs.
"And who are you?"

"Sir Ajax Lynley of Buckinghamshire."

"Buckinghamshire?" Windle glanced at Lynley's pistol lying on his black cloak by the hearth. He turned a skeptical gaze on Emily. "And you? His sister, perhaps?"

"His fiancée," said Emily levelly. "We were on the road to Dover and stopped at Lord Strayde's request to see the state of the parsonage. Unfortunately, a pair of ruffians had broken in, and attacked Lynley until he was able to fire his weapon."

"Hmm," he said, examining Lynley's arm with a gentleness at odds with his heavy frown. "The ball seems to have gone cleanly through. As you're the sort to wear clean linen, you probably have little to fear from infection. Did you lose much blood?"

Emily showed Windle the wadded neckcloth. He nodded.

"Replenish the lost fluids," he said.

He produced a glass and looked closely at the wound. With a sharp blade he cut away a fine layer of skin around the two openings. He fashioned a dressing and tied it neatly around Lynley's arm. He returned his instruments to his bag and issued a series of orders to Lynley to open and close his fist, bend his elbow, and slowly raise the injured arm. Finally, he probed the bruises on Lynley's torso. "I find no broken ribs. You're lucky."

"What may I give him?" Emily asked.

"Broth, and I'll leave you a saline draught for the pain." Windle snapped his bag closed and faced them, looking grave.

"And what may we give you for your services?" she asked. She had little money with her, but when Goldsworthy returned, they could offer more.

"That depends," he said. He pointed to Lynley's gun. "That's a dueling pistol, young man, and a damned fine one, if I'm any judge. And I'm told that the only gentleman in Buckinghamshire who wears a black cloak and a black hat is a highwayman. I've a mind to call the magistrate."

While Emily was considering how to answer him, a carriage pulled up at the door. Goldsworthy's voice boomed a greeting, and his heavy tread sounded in the passage.

Dr. Windle gaped when Goldsworthy filled the doorway and squeezed into the parlor with his treelike bulk.

"Yer the sawbones, are you?" he said. "How's my lad?"

"Should be locked up, if you ask me," said Windle. "There's some havey-cavey business going on here."

"Lock up Lynley?" Goldsworthy crossed to Lynley's side and put a huge hand on his good shoulder. "Every Englishman should drink to his health. He just saved us from going to war."

Lynley looked up. "You got the papers then?"

"It was just as you thought. Walhouse took a wood splinter in the arm from your shot. That and the weather slowed him down. Only got as far as Cuxton. Nabbed him nursing his woes over a bit of punch in the landlord's private room."

"And the papers?"

"The shah's letters to the prince were in Walhouse's traveling case, every last one."

"Now, see here," said the doctor, drawing himself up to face Goldsworthy. Emily found the room very full of men and their assumptions.

"Broth," she said to Lynley.

Offering her love a cup, Emily left the men to sort their differences and slipped away to the little barn. She found and lit a lamp from her candle, and turned her attention to Sultan.

She removed his saddle and bridle, pumped water into a pail for him, and began to brush him down with what tools she could find. She stood in the murky barn stroking the silky coat, talking to the stallion about Lynley, explaining their partnership, and feeling the horse begin to relax under her hands.

"You've missed him and fretted about him, haven't you?" she asked. "He'll mend," she promised.

When she returned, Goldsworthy had convinced the doctor to accept that they were on the side of law and order, and to take Wilde with him to procure them a chaise for their return to London. The idyll of seduction was over.

* * * *

In the morning Goldsworthy delivered Emily to her father's London house, saw her in the door with his oversized courtesy, and took Lynley away, because he could, because Lynley was a spy in the service of his country before he was the fiancé of some spoiled London miss who had had little to trouble or vex her in nearly twenty-nine years of existence, but who must now learn patience.

She went at once to beg her father's forgiveness for the worry she knew she had caused him.

It was only when she stood before him, as he sat staring unseeing at his newspaper in the morning room, his food untouched, that she realized the awkwardness of her position. There would be no explaining that she had been part of a vital mission to recover missing letters from the ruler of Persia to his son. In Russian hands, those letters, which detailed the military arrangements on which Persia depended as Russia threatened, could involve England in a war to defend Persia.

"Papa," she said. "I'm home."

He started and looked up at her, his expression rapidly shifting from glad relief to stern disapproval.

"Do you know how worried, how distraught, how wretched we've been, not knowing where you were?"

"I do, and I am sorry to have caused such distress."

"But wherever have you been?"

Emily took a deep breath. As long as she and Lynley had been together, she had not felt any fatigue, but now a great weariness washed over her, threatening to buckle her knees. "I went to find Lynley."

"Am I to understand, Emily, that in defiance of all sense and propriety, you pursued this man and his...lover across the English countryside for two days?"

"Papa, Lynley did not run away with Lady Ravenhurst."

"He never came to your engagement party. He left you to be embarrassed by the most scandalous rumor circulating around London."

Emily nodded. She wished she could say that he was on government business, saving the nation from war. "It will turn out that everyone was misled by rumor. No doubt Lady Ravenhurst was called away to her family just as Mama went to Grandmama. And no one will wonder at my absence. Everyone knows I was there for the birth of Roz's baby."

"And what of Lynley? What excuses him for leaving you?"

"He has apologized to me."

"Apologized to you! I should horsewhip him for the insult to my daughter."

Emily smiled at her father's desire to protect her. "I think I should marry him at once, Papa."

"We'll see what your mother has to say to that when she returns."

Chapter Twenty-Four

In the public mind, such is our world, a wedding's brilliance may always be measured in the quantity of lace and white satin, the number of attendants accompanying the bride, and the number of fashionable people crowding the church. However, in the minds of those most nearly concerned, who find themselves transformed by the love they've found, and who embark on a journey together in the course of which each hopes to grow more worthy of the other's love, the true measure of the ceremony's worth lies in the perfect felicity of the union.

—*The Husband Hunter's Guide to London*

Emily slept through the day. Light was fading from the sky when Alice, her maid, roused her. A number of notes had arrived for her as she slept. She had a bath and a bite to eat, and feeling moderately refreshed, sat at her desk to answer the most pressing of her correspondence.

She wrote first to Roz to assure her sister that she and Lynley were safe and sound, and to beg to come round to see and hold her sweet nephew.

She wrote to Lady Silsden to encourage her to disregard any rumor that connected Lynley to either of the Ravenhursts and to inform her that Lynley was safe and that she could expect to attend their wedding soon.

And with perfect satisfaction she wadded into tight balls those notes filled with rumors of Lynley's duel and his liaison with Lady Ravenhurst.

It took longer to write to her mother. First she went in search of the little blue and gold book that had started her on the path to adventure. She read its closing pages again and took up her pen.

Dear Mama,

I hope this letter finds Grandmama much recovered, and you relieved to see her so. You must be gladdened to hear such a happy report from Roz and Phil about the birth of their son.
I haven't thanked you properly for giving me The Husband Hunter's Guide to London. *Though I have always had you and Papa as models of what a husband and wife may be to one another, your little blue book opened my eyes about husbands and changed my thinking about what to look for in a partner for my life.*
You will, perhaps, have heard some wild, and really quite baseless, rumors about Lynley and me. I am sorry for any distress such talk may have caused you; however, considering the source of such reports, you will understand that none possesses a grain of truth. Lynley and I get on much as we have from our first meeting.
I do have a favor to ask of you as Lynley and I anticipate setting up a household together. Do you think we could have that green damask sofa you gave to Roz? It would perfectly fit our plan of decoration.

Your loving daughter,
Emily

* * * *

The next afternoon, feeling much restored in body and spirit, Emily went to see how Roz and Phil and the baby were doing. She sat with Roz in a sunny corner of Roz's bedroom, while, against common practice, Roz put the baby to her breast. Roz explained with a blush how much she delighted in the closeness with her baby and how he went from eating to sleeping and back again. She sounded so competent, so knowledgeable about her child that Emily again marveled at her sister.

"He's demanding then," Emily said as she watched her tiny nephew doze off in his mother's arms. Roz had a happy tired look, but a tired look nonetheless.

"Very, but he will sleep now for an hour or more."

"Then you should, too. Let me take him while you rest."

"Would you like to, Em?"

"I would. I'll leave you to yourself and call the nurse if I need help with him."

Roz agreed, and Emily took up her sleeping nephew and descended to Roz's drawing room. The body, she thought, continued to offer unexpected pleasures like the feel of a trusting babe asleep on one's chest.

She stared at the back of the green damask sofa and lost track of time trying to fix in her mind the impressions of the previous two weeks. After a little time, however, she realized that the sofa had been restored to its original place in the room, and that it was occupied. Her heart gave a little skip, and the sleeping babe jerked his arm and settled again.

Emily rose slowly, her legs a bit shaky under her, and crossed the room to peek over the sofa back.

Lynley looked up at her with a grin. "I knew you'd come here." He rolled to his feet and stood. "I've been to see your father," he said. "You and I have some business to attend to." He looked solemn.

"Oh?"

"And—" He reached for her hand. She lifted it from the baby and Lynley guided her back to her seat. He held her hand a moment longer to remove the ring he had given her a fortnight earlier. She didn't cry out, though her hand felt instantly bereft.

"I'm going to propose again," he said, kneeling down on one knee, still holding her hand. "I've compromised you irreparably. Even I know that. But that's not the reason I'm proposing."

"It's not?"

"No. This time I'm proposing because I love you wholly, completely, without reserve." He looked very solemn. "You are necessary to my happiness."

Emily's heart skipped in little country-dance steps of joy. The baby turned his head against her chest. Lynley spoke of happiness, and she knew he would not do so if he had not driven away the demons of the past. She smiled encouragingly.

"I want you to be my partner in life," he went on, "long after we finish catching spies."

"Are we going to catch more spies?"

"We are. You made a strong impression on Goldsworthy. He's willing to admit you as the first female spy in the club."

"I'll have assignments?"

"We will," he insisted. "As partners."

"And? There's something you're not telling me."

"Well, you do have to agree never to write to the *Times* about the club."

"I see." She looked down at her hand in his large, strong one.

He gave her hand a little shake. "Can we get back to the matter before us?"

"Which is?"

"My proposal. Will you marry me?"

"Yes."

He slipped the ring back on her finger and stood, leaning down to kiss her over the sleeping baby. The kiss was full of longing and promise. When he broke it, he glanced at the sofa.

Emily blushed to understand him. "We can't," she said.

"That doesn't stop me from wanting to," he said. "When does the baby go back to his mother?"

"When he needs her," Emily said firmly.

"I'll wait." He dropped a light kiss on her cheek, and flashed a grin at her before he disappeared once more behind the high arching back of the sofa.

Emily kissed the baby's head. "Would you like a cousin?" she whispered. "I think it can be arranged."

After a time of perfect contentment in which the diamonds on Emily's ring winked up at her and the sleeping baby breathed against the lace at her collarbone, the drawing room door opened. A businesslike rustle of skirts sounded, and Emily's mother came to a halt, looking down her.

"Hello, Mama," Emily said. "Roz is having a rest."

"Emily dear, I'm quite confused. Are you engaged or not?"

"Very much engaged, Mama." Emily smiled over her nephew's little head.

Her mother looked harassed and skeptical. "Your father seemed to think that your betrothal was a jest, and he had no idea what to make of your continuing it after your fiancé did not attend your engagement party."

"Oh, Mama, I have a great deal to tell you, and I do have to thank you for the little blue book. Will you sit down? Should I ring for tea?"

Her mother sat opposite her. "But what is he like? How can there have been all these rumors?"

"You shall meet him presently, Mama, and see that other than his height, which is a little out of the ordinary, and his habit, acquired I believe in Spain, of napping where no one may detect him in the middle of the day, he is a most respectable young man."

From the green sofa came Lynley's laugh, warm and happy. "Enough," he said, coming to his full height and bowing, as Emily's mother gaped at him.

"She's roasting you, ma'am, as you'll see when we become better acquainted."

"Oh my," said her mother. "You are tall."

Lynley dropped a kiss on Emily's head. "I will let your daughter tell you all about us, ma'am. And"—he turned back to Emily—"will you come for a drive with me tomorrow, Em? There's something I wish to show you."

Emily nodded and hid a smile as her mother gaped after Lynley's retreating form.

"Mama, Roz will be down in a moment. Do you want to hold the baby?"

"I'm dying to," said her mother.

Epilogue

My dear husband hunter, if you are reading this page, I must thank you for your attention to my small volume. It is my hope that its lessons will serve you well. Perhaps you have come to see that happiness in marriage is not entirely a matter of chance, but rather that young women and men of sense and character may so conduct themselves in this great million-peopled city of ours as to find the sort of lasting love that makes a great joy of the marriage union.

—*The Husband Hunter's Guide to London*

They married on the morning of Emily's twenty-ninth birthday. Lynley and Emily left the small family breakfast that followed their nuptials, in a chaise and four bound for a brief wedding trip.

"There's a place I'd like you to see," he said simply as he handed her into the chaise.

As they traveled, he held her hand and gave her further details of Walhouse's capture and the restoration of the missing papers. It seemed a lazy journey. Emily felt no impatience. She understood him better now. The tangled feelings that had driven him to help Lady Ravenhurst did not arise from the lady's beauty but only from her resemblance to the woman who had betrayed his boyish faith in love.

Emily watched him to see how he held himself and how he adjusted to the movement of the chaise. If she felt any impatience, it was only to know about the state of his wounds. He had joked that they might make use of the green sofa, but she did not know what their wedding night held.

Before midday they left the main Aylesbury Road and shortly reached a lodge at the gated entrance to an avenue lined with tall beeches. The lodgekeeper admitted them, and at length a view opened up, and she could see an expanse of lawn before a sprawling gray stone house. He now watched her with some trepidation.

"It's Lyndale, isn't it?" she asked. "Your home. It's lovely."

The coachman pulled the chaise to a stop at the entrance, and a proper butler emerged from the columned portico to usher them inside. Emily was conscious of a bustle of servants and a babble of tongues, not only English, but something else.

She admired the soaring, light-filled entrance hall and grand staircase. "My father will approve," she said.

"Do you?" he asked.

She nodded.

"Come," he said, his face sober.

He led the way, and they stepped into another room, as dark as the entry was light, its walls lined with crimson damask and hung with paintings, its velvet drapery pulled closed. A white wainscot ran around the base of the walls, but the whole impression was of gloom and suffering.

Beside her Lynley had gone quiet. She moved to examine the paintings on the nearest wall. In front of her were three saints undergoing martyrdom or agonizing distress—one shot with arrows, another fasting in the desert, a third fleeing persecution.

She glanced at him. He waved her on. She moved down the length of the impressively long room, looking up at saints and sinners in torment or exile, and she could not help but notice the flaw in Lady Silsden's plan of moral instruction.

When she had dutifully completed her circuit of the room, examining every painting, and returned to Lynley, she could not hide a smile and a bit of impatience.

"Lynley," she said, waving a hand to indicate the splendid collection of art, "was this your aunt's idea of quelling your...natural instincts?"

He nodded. She took him by the hand and led him to stand in front of the first painting she'd examined. "That explains her failure then. How could she hope to repress your earthly desires while surrounding you with such a display of flesh? They're all quite naked, you know."

She tugged him by the neckcloth and pushed his jaw up to examine the first of the paintings. "Look at this fellow dressed only in his halo." She pointed to the next one. "And that one, who seems to have got his neckcloth around his nether parts."

She waited, watching as quick comprehension sprang up in his eyes. Then he let out a laugh, a great gust of joy released from long constraint. He picked her up and waltzed her madly around the great room in defiance of all the gloom and suffering on its walls.

When he set her on her feet again, breathless and trembling, she looked up into his happy gaze and reached up to touch his imperfect mouth—and chose the future.

"Lynley, I'm ready for you to get me out of my clothes. Now."

Upstairs in another red-damasked room with a long-dead pope looking down on them from above a white marble mantel, they made a laughing ceremony of undressing each other and fell into the bed.

And Emily discovered that the paintings hardly told the full story of flesh, for one could only look at them, and it was necessary to touch. Touch they did, shyly at first, so that Emily might notice and record in her flesh the sensation of his hands on her breasts and the pull deep in her belly, then more boldly, her hands moving as freely as his, their flesh warm and slick and sliding together, sensations coming fast, like dozens of bells taking up a peal, setting the air trembling and quivering, until an urgent need she had never known left her open and clinging to him.

He held himself above her, and shifted so that his shaft slid across the entrance of her slick cleft. Emily lifted her hips to meet his. A shudder wracked them both.

"Now?" he asked.

She arched up to kiss him. "Lynley, my spy, my love. Know that I mean to seduce you every day of our married life."

He laughed and together they broke that last of the barriers between them.

"You must remind me," he said much later as they lay skin to skin, "to thank my aunt for a perfect education."

* * * *

A fortnight after his return to London from his wedding trip, Lynley, with Phil at his side, tracked Barksted down at his club. Lord and Lady Ravenhurst had left town for their principle estate in the country, and the contradictory rumors about Lady Ravenhurst's earlier absence from London had largely cancelled each other out. Everyone suspected an unhappy marriage and a lover, but with the announcement of Lynley's marriage to Lady Emily Radstock, even those gentlemen inclined to bet on the identity of Lady Ravenhurst's secret lover, would not take odds on Lynley.

The shah's missing letters to his son had been restored to the Foreign Office. War with Russia had been averted. In custody and facing trial for treason, Walhouse had spoken quite openly about his activities. In exchange for his cooperation, he would not be hanged, but transported. Even Walhouse, however, did not know who remained of Malikov's spy ring. Somewhere in London an enemy continued to look for the weak links in the Foreign Office's handling of confidential information. Once wed, Lynley and his lady, for Emily Radstock would be his lady, would hunt spies together.

Lynley found the prospect of working with his bride energizing. She had promised to seduce him every night of their married life, and a certain green and peony damask sofa figured in his thoughts of how that seduction might proceed.

There was just one unfinished piece of business in what Goldsworthy was calling the Ravenhurst affair, and Lynley had come to the club to settle that purely personal score. Barksted had failed with Lady Ravenhurst. However disillusioned she might be, she had returned to her husband. But unless someone stopped him, Barksted would remain the kind of man who, like the Russian who had seduced Lynley's mother, would use and discard a woman, pushing her farther down the path to ruin.

The interior of Barksted's club was much like the coffee room of the Pantheon Club, with a high barrel ceiling, hanging chandeliers, and tall windows covered with velvet drapery. Unlike the Pantheon Club coffee room, however, the room at Barksted's club was devoted to green baize gaming tables, which lined the wall under the windows.

At the second table Lynley found Barksted, a pile of winnings in front of him, a desperate young man slouched opposite, and three other players wearing looks of boredom or disgust. He knew none of the other men, but two of them nodded to Phil.

"Barksted, I have a debt to settle with you," Lynley announced.

Barksted turned with a lazy sneer. "Slunk back to London, have you?"

Lynley seized Barksted by his lapels, lifted him from his chair, set him on his feet in the middle of the patterned carpet, and stepped back. Play at the surrounding tables stopped. Waiters paused in their movements.

"You may put up your fists, Barksted, if you think you are man enough to face another in a fair fight." Lynley gave the word *fair* its due emphasis. He suspected Barksted had never played fairly in his life.

"You're mad, Lynley. You can't come into a gentleman's club and insult a member."

"Ah, but you are no gentleman, are you, Barksted?" Lynley paused. "You're a mawworm who preys on women. If you won't fight, you'll have to take the punishment you deserve."

Barksted looked around as if some friend or ally would come to his assistance, but no one spoke up. He shrugged his shoulders.

"Do your worst, Lynley. I seem to remember that you always end up on the losing end of a fight."

Lynley delivered a direct hit to Barksted's jaw from a purposeful left, sending the man to the floor. "For using a woman's gaming debts to separate her from her husband and children."

Phil picked the floored gentleman up and set him on his feet. Barksted wobbled, his hand to his jaw. "You are..."

"Left-handed? So I am." Again, Lynley's left fist flashed out, this time colliding with Barksted's nose. There was a notable crack and a spray of blood as Barksted went down. "For letting your henchman lay a hand on my lady."

Barksted did not rise. He lifted his neckcloth to his gushing nose. His friends turned back to their gaming.

Lynley stood over his fallen enemy. "Remain in London if you like, Barksted, but never annoy a woman again."

Dear Reader,

The slim blue volume with gold lettering, entitled **The Husband Hunter's Guide to London,** *first fell into the hands of Jane Fawkener, who takes it as a clue behind her father's disappearance…*

Read on for a preview of Kate Moore's first Husband Hunter's Guide to London, available now.

Every unmarried gentlewoman who comes to London for the Season must accept that finding a husband is the business of her life. Neither her family nor society offers any other honorable provision for her future. Therefore, until she forms an attachment with a man of respectable family, decent habits, and comfortable income, a sensible woman will make use of every available means to put herself in the way of eligible parties and will devote her time and her energies to determining who among them is both suitable for the purpose and susceptible to her charms. To waste even a single evening in idle flirtation or to pin one's hopes on unreasonable expectations is to risk no less a thing of lasting value than her own happiness. The purpose of this slim volume, then, is to guide the Husband Hunter through the perilous waters of the Season to the calm shores of wedded life.

—*The Husband Hunter's Guide to London*

Chapter One

Jane Fawkener looked up from the little blue book in her hands at the two solemn gentlemen seated opposite her in the office of her father's bank. The book's title in ornate gilt script must be a joke, a cruel joke. Surely, she had not journeyed a quarter of the way around the globe for news of her father only to receive the little blue volume.

She found it difficult to breathe, some pressure squeezing her chest, not just the unfamiliar stays. She had come to the bank straight from the Foreign Office where Lord Chartwell, the official in charge of the near East, had shared with her a letter her father had written to his cousin Teddy Walhouse. Chartwell had no letter for her. She had known better than to expect one from her father through such a compromised channel, but from her father's bankers, his most private and secure means of communication, she had expected a letter of her own. Not a book, and certainly not this book.

She turned the worn little volume over in her hands. "Marry? My father wants me to marry?" She tried to keep her voice steady.

Both men nodded with grave and awkward sympathy. She was unaccustomed to pale English faces, but she did not detect in either man any of the signs of duplicity or avarice her father had trained her to recognize, nor any of the indifference with which Lord Chartwell had met her inquiries earlier.

George Hammersley, the older gentleman, had blunt, sober features and black hair peppered with gray, while his son Frank had a youthful, open face in which the same features were softened and refined, but contracted by just a pinch of pain in the expression. The younger man leaned heavily on a cane whenever he stood.

She wondered what they made of her. She did not recognize herself in her borrowed mourning clothes. Before her ship docked, a pair of well-intentioned lady missionaries who had been in Greece to bring translations of the Bible to the warring factions there, had taken her aside and helped her to dress for her arrival in London. Today she wore her first stays, laced tight under three layers of petticoats, and a heavy black gown of a dull, stiff fabric. Her usual clothes, her loose pants and bright tunics, lay folded in her trunk.

George Hammersley cleared his throat. "Miss Fawkener, an entail of this sort is very common in England to keep an estate within a family, but your father's will does authorize us to provide two hundred pounds for your use until such time as you…marry."

Jane regarded the book in her hands. It could not be all that remained of her father. She could understand why he had not written to her through the Foreign Office, but she could not fathom why he had not sent her a direct message through his bankers. With what composure she could muster, she refrained from flinging the little book on the glowing fire in the grate. It surely deserved all the curses of Arabia.

May you crumble into dust finer than the smallest grains of sand in the desert, may weary asses and camels grind you underfoot, and may the four winds blow the specks of you to the ends of the earth.

Silently, she sent the curse into the fire-warmed air of the office, and wished it up the chimney flue and out into the sky. Her father was missing somewhere along the vast mysterious network of trade and intrigue from the Mediterranean to the Himalayas. The British Foreign Office, which had swooped her up from her father's house in Halab and hustled her onto a ship in Koron Harbor, now refused to help her discover his fate. Instead they promised to bestow upon her father a knighthood and a piece of shining silver that meant nothing. He would be *Sir* George Fawkener, *deceased*. Lord Chartwell had turned from her to the paperwork on his desk as if he had already forgotten the existence of her father and expected her to do the same.

But it was impossible to forget one had a father, that he had taught her Greek and Arabic and taken her with him everywhere, that he had been endlessly funny and energetic and reckless and brave, that he'd had crinkles around his clever blue eyes, did magic tricks with his big hands, and filled his pockets with almonds and pistachios.

She had been delayed at the dock while some customs matter was resolved, and while someone apparently searched her trunk. Her father's previous letters remained in her possession, but she recognized from the alteration in the ribbon with which they were tied, that the bundle had been opened. Someone in London was spying on her.

In those circumstances she had felt an unreasonable burst of hope a few moments earlier when the Hammersleys produced a brown-paper package from her father. Whatever he sent through them had escaped the scrutiny of his enemies. But all hope of a personal message from him had died when she unwrapped the little book. Her father had washed his hands of her. Her head felt like mush while her heart felt squeezed in her chest. She stared down at the little book lying on the voluminous folds of her black skirts.

A moment of dizziness overcame her. She was not at sea, not bobbing and dipping in an unsettled way over vast gray waters, but in the grip of an odd uneasiness that had started the moment she stepped off the ship.

The cursed book remained clutched in her hand. She was far from any desert where camels might trample it underfoot. She flipped it open, looking for a message, a word in her father's looping scrawl, but there was no inscription, no hint of his intention. There was, however, a map, folded inside the front cover, along the interior edge of the book's binding. She opened its folds, a map of London in watercolor pale greens, pinks, and browns with the great blue ribbon of the river, the Thames, snaking through it.

She straightened her spine. The map meant there was more to his message than the unexpected advice to marry. His bankers might believe him dead. The Foreign Office might believe it, but Jane refused to believe he was dead without confirmation. After all, he had only gone on one of the trips he had been making for the British government for nine years. He'd always come back before. She just had to figure out what he meant by leaving her the little guide. It had to be one of her father's games, a game she could learn to play.

She closed the book. When she looked up, the motion again triggered that feeling that she was at sea with her chair pitching under her like a rowboat in rough swells.

Frank Hammersley watched her face. "Miss Fawkener, the Foreign Office is sending a protocol officer to take charge of you, but as we are a little ahead of our time, may I bring you a restorative? A glass of wine, perhaps?"

She lifted a hand to refuse the wine, wishing she could refuse the Foreign Office functionary as well. A flock of questions stirred in her head, but the two earnest gentlemen across from her did not look the least bit ready to answer them. They both jumped at a light knock on the office door.

A striking young woman, with a merry face framed by glossy black ringlets, and figure that announced her to be with child, stopped abruptly midstride, looking abashed for interrupting.

"Oh, I beg your pardon. I didn't realize you two were with a client."

"Come in, Violet, my dear." The elder Mr. Hammersley hurried to her side as if she might escape. "You may be able to help us if Miss Fawkener is willing to share her circumstances with you. Miss Fawkener, my daughter, Lady Violet Blackstone."

Smiling, Lady Violet turned to Jane and offered her hand. "Hello. Have these two bankers offended you, Miss Fawkener?"

Jane shook her head cautiously. "Not at all. It's merely that..."

Frank Hammersley chimed in, leaning on his cane. "It's merely that the subject of marriage came up, and two males found themselves of no help in the matter."

Lady Violet turned a bright, curious gaze on Jane. "Oh dear, how awkward for you. If you would feel more at ease talking with me, we could retire to my office. I have a friend with me at present. We were about to take tea, if you'd care to join us."

"You have an office here?" Jane could not help her surprise.

Lady Violet's eyes brightened. "I do, the privilege of being a banker's daughter. Shall we go? I'll call for some tea, or would you prefer wine?"

"Tea, thank you." She did not ask for coffee. The English did not drink it as she would at home from a copper pot hot off the fire with a rich sweet foam on top of the tiny cup.

"When you are refreshed, you may share as much as you like with me. I will treat anything you say in the strictest confidence, of course."

Frank Hammersley offered Jane his hand, and she rose, still clutching the book. "My sister will take good care of you, Miss Fawkener, and we'll look out for your visitor from the Foreign Office."

Jane thanked him and took her leave of the two gentlemen. She followed Lady Violet to another office, less grand and austere than the first, but with a businesslike desk in spite of some feminine touches. Seated on a small sofa was an elegant lady a few years older than Lady Violet, who introduced her friend as Her Grace the Duchess of Huntingdon.

The lady with the bright green eyes and Titian hair laughed. "Violet likes to announce my title, but believe me, I'm just her copper 'Penny' when we are having a heart-to-heart talk."

Lady Violet and Jane settled in pretty blue and white chinoiserie wing chairs, opposite the sofa, and Jane let the friends talk until tea arrived. Lady Violet made a face at a pair of round, flowered pots. "I'm afraid I'm only permitted herbal tea these days, Miss Fawkener, but you and Penny may have some of this lovely bohea."

With a steaming cup in her hands and under the influence of her new companions' easy manners, Jane found herself explaining her dependence on certain funds, which she could only obtain, according to her father's will, by marrying. She did not mention the Foreign Office's interference in her affairs. At the word *entail* both ladies shook their heads.

"And you find that you are not conveniently in love with some eligible gentleman?" The Duchess shook her head. "I'm afraid that puts you at the mercy of the London marriage mart." She spoke with a sympathetic frankness that warmed Jane as much as the tea.

"I admit I don't know the first thing about getting on in London, let alone finding a husband here. But surely a woman doesn't find a husband with a guidebook?" She hefted the little book in her hand.

Lady Violet raised one dark brow. "I suspect that many a miss would consume that volume quite eagerly. You've no enthusiasm for the hunt?"

"Only to know how fast it may be done," Jane confessed. Her throat ached in spite of the comforting tea. She needed money to search for her father, but marrying to gain money would mean accepting that her father was truly gone.

Lady Violet put down her tea. "All you have from your father is this guidebook? May I see it?"

Jane passed the book to her.

A tiny crease appeared on Lady Violet's brow as she opened the book and read its title page. Her eyes flashed with interest as if she were trying to solve a puzzle. "I wonder what your father was thinking, Miss Fawkener? Presumably, from your knowledge of his character, you can see some hint of his intention. We must assume that he has your best interest at heart, but even to acquire certain funds, a hasty marriage hardly seems the sort of thing a wise father would advise."

"But fathers rule, don't they?" Her grace commented with a wistful laugh. "In my experience a dead father's will has a powerful influence on a living daughter's life." She looked embarrassed at the strength of her opinion and turned to their hostess. "Violet, I really must take my leave and let you get to the bottom of this dear girl's situation with all the privacy you need. But"—she turned to Jane, her eyes alight now with mirth—"I can offer one service I know to be of value to the husband hunter—an invitation to one of my Thursday evening gatherings. You may depend on me in this matter, Miss Fawkener."

Lady Violet saw her friend out. Jane heard their parting laughter and it struck her that the lady missionaries on board ship, who had lent her the proper clothes to wear, had not laughed. At the time Jane had not recognized the lack, but now she realized how strange it had been not to laugh.

Lady Violet returned and settled in the blue chair, refreshing both their cups of tea. "My friend, Penny, has a great deal of influence in the fashionable world, and I think you'll find her sincere in her offer."

Of one thing Jane was sure. If her father wanted her to have the book, and if he had used his bankers rather than the Foreign Office to get the book into her hands, she needed to find its hidden meaning. Once her world stopped rocking unreasonably, she would study the cursed book again.

After a moment of silent contemplation, Lady Violet spoke. "Miss Fawkener, whatever you decide, your confidences are safe with me, but tell me, what are your immediate plans?"

"I've been advised to take rooms at Mivart's Hotel."

"You do not go to your family then?" Lady Violet did not conceal her surprise.

"None opened their doors." It was one of the difficulties of Jane's situation. She had no *wasta* as her neighbors in Halab would call it, no person in a position of influence to support her cause. The English consul in Halab had simply turned her over to the Foreign Office, and no one there wished to do a thing for her father.

Lady Violet made a sympathetic murmur. "Mivart's costs can be quite steep. You'll need additional funds. Have you any?"

"You think my two hundred pounds will not permit a hotel stay of any length?"

Violet looked grave for the first time in their conversation. "It might get you through months of frugal living in London, but it will last less than a fortnight at Mivart's. The hotel will charge you for each bag a footman carries, the number of coals on your fire, and who knows what else."

"I see." Jane set down her tea. The hotel would consume the money she needed to launch the search for her father.

"Do not despair." Violet reached out and gave Jane's hand a squeeze. "As your bankers, we would be remiss if we did not help you reduce your expenses. You must have time in which to decide the future partner of your life. We also have the resources to...how shall I say it...investigate any gentleman not fully known to your family. Now, what may I do for you straightaway? I'm afraid you've been taken here and there, subjected to our government's high-handedness, when what you most need is time to restore your powers."

An aching lump rose in Jane's throat at the unexpected kindness. "Thank you. I'd like to go to the hotel, if I may."

"Of course." Lady Violet stood. "You may wait to thank me, for I must warn you I can be of no very great help should you wish to pursue a match as *The Husband Hunter's Guide* recommends. In the eyes of polite society, as a *banker's* daughter, I've trespassed on exalted territory in marrying Lord Blackstone, a peer. I've only escaped total censure because Blackstone himself was considered too scandalous and too impoverished for a noble bride."

Jane watched her companion. The lady's eyes sparkled happily. "Of course, I suspect that sometimes, the least eligible gentlemen make the most remarkable husbands."

About the Author

Kate Moore is a former English teacher and three-time RITA finalist, and Golden Heart and Book Buyers Best award winner. She writes Austen-inspired fiction set in nineteenth-century England or contemporary California. Her heroes are men of courage, competence, and unmistakable virility, with determination so strong it keeps their sensuality in check until they meet the right woman. Her heroines take on the world with practical good sense and kindness to bring those heroes into a circle of love and family. Sometimes there's even a dog. Kate lives north of San Francisco with her surfer husband, their yellow Lab, a Pack 'n Play for visiting grandbabies, and miles of crowded bookshelves. Kate's family and friends offer endless support and humor. Her children are her best works, and her husband is her favorite hero. Visit Kate at Facebook.com/KateMooreAuthor or contact her at kate@katemoore.com.

CPSIA information can be obtained
at www.ICGtesting.com
Printed in the USA
LVHW091215220319
611421LV00008B/222/P

9 781516 101795